At the Boundary Between Daylight and Shadow

A STORY OF THE SEVEN WORLD DOMINION

EILEEN R HICKMAN

SHADOWED WORD PRESS

To John
You've been waiting a long time,
never wavering in your support.
Thank you!

Enjoy More of Eileen R Hickman's Stories

To get the updates on new stories in the Seven World Dominion, sign up for Eileen's monthly newsletter at www.eileenrhickman.com. As a thankyou gift, you'll receive the free story, *Dragon Light*, which introduces you to the first world in the Dominion, Sek-Nar.

But wait! There's more. When you've finished reading *At The Boundary of Daylight and Shadow* continue on to the back matter where you'll find the short story *Tendrils of Shadow*. *Tendrils* is set on Luxera, the second world of Seven World Dominion, the world of the Light Spinners. Yours to enjoy as a bonus gift from Eileen.

Contents

1

FIRE AND ASH

Just before dawn, the safehouse on Sutton Street burned. An imposing old house from the prewar era, it stood proudly for six hundred years watching the city develop into a technological hub and then slip into decay. Now, in little more than an hour, under the ministrations of greedy flames, it was reduced to a pile of ash. The fire department came too late and concentrated on trying to save the houses on either side.

Ranita, watching the building in its final death throes from across and down the street, groaned as the roof fell with a crash and an eruption of flame. She turned her body away when the front wall tumbled with a loud whoosh and a shower of sparks, though she kept her head angled back toward the conflagration, unable to avert her gaze. But when the side walls gave way, she dug her fingers into eyes stinging from smoke, unable to watch any longer.

Some of her people were there, buried in the ash and debris. New recruits to the resistance program, they had come to the house with the promise of safety. A few escaped with the handlers. Too few.

The First Ministry had raided in the darkest hour, when sleep claimed even those tasked with protection. Its agents did their work with brutal efficiency. The First Ministry was always most efficient when it detected a threat to its absolute power.

Ranita got word of the raid too late to raise a warning. There was time only for a frantic rushing of terrified recruits out the back door as the First Ministry Agents, Dark Spinners wrapped in shifting tendrils of shadow, entered at the front. And after that, the screams, suddenly cut off, that told her anyone left behind was beyond rescue. Or so she thought until she scouted around to the front in time to see Dark Spinners haul three people into the street before wrapping them in shadow and spinning away.

Ranita recognized one. Jacob. An older man. She had spent a year recruiting him. Now he was in the hands of the First Ministry.

A strong-spirited man, he might withstand the interrogation. For a while anyway. But not forever. Did he know enough to cause actual damage to the home community?

She wasn't sure, and she didn't know the identities of the other two who were taken. Their faces had been shrouded by shadow. A man and a woman. That was all she knew.

Now the First Ministry agents were gone. The fire department doused what was left of the house's sides to keep smoldering embers from igniting nearby buildings. All that was left of home and hearth, bones and flesh, was ash and smoke.

The citizens of Skakeet City, heading to work, slowed for a moment as they passed the remains of the house. Their faces reflected recognition, and with the recognition, a flash of fear. But they quickly buried the fear and adjusted facial expressions, sometimes making furtive checks of fellow pedestrians to see if anyone had noticed the moment of weakness. They continued up the street with bright demeanors firmly in place, exhibiting a false eagerness to get to their jobs. Hurrying to serve their dark masters.

The ruins would act as a deterrent to anyone who might have recruitment potential. The First Ministry understood this. It gave them a reason to burn, as if they needed a reason. As if their joy in wanton destruction would not have been sufficient excuse for fire and smoke.

Ranita shifted, letting her shoulder blades scrape along the rough surface of the wall she leaned against, welcoming the discomfort. Her work would be harder now. Few would have the courage to join the resistance with a smoldering ruin bearing witness to the danger.

She recruited with the promise of safety and then spent every waking moment trying to ensure that safety. It was her work in life. The reason she powered up her skimmer every morning. But somewhere, something had gone wrong this time.

Ranita's skin tingled on the underside of her right wrist. Control was signaling for her to report in. She gave the smoldering rubble one last hard look before starting up the street, matching her stride to the businesslike pace of the growing crowd.

Across the street, a Dark Spinner sauntered in the direction of the ruin. His gait, his demeanor, suggested lack of purpose, but he didn't fool Ranita, or anyone else on the street. The humans sharing the walkway with him left a wide space open all around him. Dark Spinners didn't frequent this area without a reason.

Ranita gave him a swift appraisal. His pale skin and magenta hair set him apart from the human populace. He was even taller than most spinners, and they were a tall race. His powerful grace marked him as a trained agent. Most telling, the swirl of shadow around his right arm signaled his readiness to form a weapon at a moment's notice.

Ranita turned her gaze away before she caught the color of his eyes. She was too far away to read anything in the swirling of his eye flecks. Those were difficult for a non-spinner to interpret, even one with Ranita's training and experience, and it wouldn't do to let him see her studying him.

She let her own gait slow to a careless shuffle and schooled her features, but blocking the heat that rose from her belly to suffuse her face was harder. A fire burned in her soul, a fire of hatred and anger that threatened to turn to smoke the light of faith she had dedicated her life to.

Ranita's face cooled as she walked, though the seething anger remained. She let the crowd carry her along until she reached the north side of the business district. Here she loitered, checking to be sure the Dark Spinner was out of sight, to be sure he hadn't followed her. Reassured, she turned down a dirty street that took her past run-down factories, where dark plumes of toxic smoke competed with the racket of machinery.

She bit hard on her lower lip and hurried by, trying not to think about the lives of those who must live and work here. She must clear her thoughts of the suffocating anger that these conditions heightened, if she wanted to be able to do her job.

On the edge of town, she entered an old park, abandoned and overgrown. It appeared deserted, and Ranita released a loud breath, relieved her skimmer remained invisible.

The machine's cloaking device had been phasing in and out. The tech at the maintenance facility had assured her he had fixed it, but she hadn't trusted him. The skimmer was too new to her, though not new in any other way. Handed down from a retired agent, it appeared ready to fall apart at the first burst of speed. Nothing like her sleek, new craft, which now rested at the bottom of the sea on the far side of the world.

Not her fault. One of the hazards of the job. Escaping a concerted Dark Spinner attack without injury was a victory, even if one of the most expensive pieces of equipment in the world was now disintegrating in sea water, undergoing a transformation that would leave it a rusted-out home for fish.

At least the vile Dark Spinners hadn't gotten their hands on it. She'd made sure of that. It had been worth the loss of the skimmer to foil her shadowy foe. But it was hard not to kick herself every time she returned to her hand-me-down ride. Maybe she should have retired after she lost the new craft.

Not that the techs hadn't done a great job overhauling the old skimmer. It operated as expected. Even the cloak remained steady since the last servicing.

A slight pressure on the controls embedded above her left wrist dropped the cloak, and the skimmer popped into view. Just under five meters in length, its sleek design almost made up for the dented and discolored plating, evidence of its hard service.

Ranita walked around the craft, inspecting it for signs of tampering, then gave her wrist control a quick double tap, triggering the door. It slid open without a sound, revealing an opening into the refurbished interior. Ignoring the step that lowered as the door activated, Ranita lifted a long leg into the compartment and pulled herself into the pilot's seat.

A quick punch on the control panel retracted the step and closed the door. Another punch reengaged the cloak. After verifying it held steady, Ranita leaned back in the seat with a sigh and rubbed her face with both hands. What should she say in her report? How could she explain what had happened, and why?

But it must be done. Best get it over with. She lowered her hands and punched in a series of codes on her control panel. A light blinked green, and she pulled the keyboard closer, ignoring the voice com controls. Typing was more impersonal than speaking. She needed impersonal right now. But before she could start, a voice sounded over the com speaker.

"Ranita Ranesh, come in, please." Ranita recognized Bithiah's voice. Bithiah supervised a cadre of agents. She didn't work the coms. She must feel communication was urgent.

Ranita tapped the com activation button to respond. "Ranita here. I was about to type in my report."

"Delay that. We've received reports from three other agents concerning the raid at Sutton house. Enough information to move forward."

"Very good. Awaiting instructions."

"First Ministry took three recruits. Identified as Jacob Winter, Willem Kolb, and Bella Montaine. Eyewitness reports place them entering the First Ministry Headquarters in Hikeet. Interrogation will follow, we presume. We must extract them before they talk."

"Agreed. What's the plan?"

"Force is unlikely to succeed. It will need to be a clandestine operation."

Ranita nodded, knowing what was coming. "Agreed. How many?"

"One."

"My gig?"

"Affirmative. Gilad is on standby for emergency extraction. Time is important, but I don't need to tell you, it's more critical to avoid apprehension than to retrieve the prisoners. Whatever they know, you know more, so keep yourself clean. The security of the entire community is at stake. We're implementing damage control protocols at this end."

No. Ranita didn't need to be reminded to keep herself free and clean. But Bithiah was nervous. Sending a single agent into any First Ministry compound was high risk, but it was the only way. Though Bithiah had the courage to give the order, that didn't mean she wouldn't overcompensate by giving needless instructions.

Ranita had been in the First Ministry Headquarters building in Hikeet several times in the past. Enough to know what a fortress it was. Her chances for success depended on where the three were being held. It wouldn't be easy, no matter what, but some areas might be impossible.

"I'll have to wait until evening to formulate a plan," she told Bithiah. "I can't reach my contacts until then, and I'll need information before I proceed."

"Understood. Take the time you need to do it right." Bithiah paused. "But not too much time." Another pause. "All mission parameters at your discretion. Maintain com silence from here on except with Gilad, and then only when necessary. Go with Ya-Lohim. Bithiah out."

Ranita sat back in her seat with a loud expulsion of her breath. Bithiah had been more succinct than expected. She and Ranita both knew there was nothing more to be said that could mitigate the risk. The mission depended solely on Ranita's wits and skills, and on the blessings of Ya-Lohim.

Ranita retrieved some field rations from a storage compartment and munched through them while she reviewed everything her data banks contained on the First Ministry Building. It wasn't enough. She hoped her contacts in Hikeet would fill in a few of the gaps.

Her review complete, she tried to sleep. She often slept in skimmers, and slept well, but today, no matter how she shifted and squirmed, she could not get comfortable, could not relax. Images came to her. The flames and the screams of Sutton Street mingled with older images. Explosions. A swirling darkness covering the advance of a phalanx of humans. The humans, shielded by their Dark Spinner masters, cut through resistance with blazing laser weapons in their hands and snarls of hate twisting their mouths. As they massacred their fellow humans, shining void ships lifted like blazing suns and disappeared into the expanse of the void.

"I've watched too many historical videos," Ranita muttered, shifting again in her seat.

And wondered again about those humans who had fled Exalton three hundred years ago. The same questions she had asked many times before. Had they survived? Where had they gone? Why couldn't her ancestors have gone with them? She might be living in a peaceful town with trees and grass and children playing. Maybe even her children.

She tried to push these thoughts from her mind before they turned to the inevitable last questions, but as always, her mind pushed through the complete cycle. To the questions agents asked each other when they gathered for training or socialization. The questions that kept them looking with hope toward the sky. The questions that kept them pushing themselves into danger every day.

Those exiles had promised to return when they gained the needed strength. To come blazing from the sky and reclaim their world from the outsiders and their mindless followers. Their promise fueled hope in the resistance community and kept them at their task through setbacks and sacrifices, even though it seemed everyday they would be exposed and destroyed, overtaken by the shadow that surrounded them.

And yet, the exiles did not return. Perhaps, would never return.

Ranita sat upright, pushing these thoughts away with an impatient flick of her wrist. She would continue to look for the exiles' return until some evidence came to dash that hope. And she would continue to put herself in danger to keep open a safe landing place for them, a safe base from which to launch the reconquest of their world.

Even more important, she would continue her efforts to reclaim Exalton for the light. She didn't need rescuers from the void to do that.

It was getting too late to sleep, even if there was any chance sleep would come. She gathered up the few things she would need and divested herself of anything she didn't need, including all clues to her identity.

She paused, tempted to take the skimmer into Hikeet. The cloak was holding steady, and the time saved would be significant. But Hikeet's security measures outmatched Skakeet City's the way even her old skimmer outmatched the capabilities of the local transports. The skimmer was safer where it was, and she wouldn't need it, since Gilad was on standby for extraction.

She opened the weapons locker and moved her hand toward the smaller of the two laser guns stored there. Her hand hovered for a moment before she pulled it back. It was easy to conceal, easy to use. And deadly.

She glanced at the other weapon. A larger piece, almost hefty enough to be considered a rifle. Though impossible to conceal, it might be useful inside the First Ministry Building if she ran into trouble. And trouble was likely.

But the weapon had just one intended function. A function she could manage without. She flipped the lid of the locker down over the weapons and secured it. It had been a long time since she carried firepower. That wasn't going to change today.

It was early yet, but she didn't want to attract attention by appearing rushed. She initiated a quick sensor sweep to prepare for leaving the skimmer. When it showed that the way was clear, she popped the skimmer's door open and slid out. A quick tap on the embedded controls closed the door and steadied the cloak.

2

—·—

HIKEET INFORMANT

An hour later, Ranita sat under a cluster of evergreen trees, watching the traffic on the road between Skakeet City and Hikeet and waiting. Waiting for dusk to gather. Waiting for the shadows to grow deep enough to hide her movements from watchful eyes. Curbing her impatience for action. Knowing her ability to avoid detection might mean the difference between life and death, not only for herself but for three other people.

She pulled images of three faces from her memory and held them in her mind, putting names to them: Jacob, Willem, and Bella. The exercise fueled her resolve but also made it harder to tamp down her impatience. Time was short, every minute crucial.

Even so, she waited.

She checked the digital timepiece she carried, but the numbers hardly registered in her mind.

15

They didn't matter. She would move when the level of daylight was right, not before.

Traffic on the road was thinning. A few private skimmers passed, most heading from Hikeet into Skakeet City. Human workers operated them, heading home after a day of bowing to every whim of their Dark Spinner employers. The public transports were still full, though no longer packed. A few headed toward Hikeet carrying night watchmen, servants heading for night duty, entertainers, and restaurant and café employees.

There were no Dark Spinners. They seldom used the road. Why sully themselves by rubbing shoulders with the human masses? They preferred to vaunt their superiority by turning themselves into shadow and spinning, at the speed of light, to their destinations.

Ranita's lips curled, the only outward sign of disgust she would allow herself. Then she shrugged, a rueful motion. She would spin too, if she had that ability. It would be foolish not to. But she hoped she'd be more sensitive than to make a flagrant display of her ability in front of those who could not spin.

The absence of Dark Spinners on the road meant no one would notice Ranita if she went to the nearest stop and hopped on a transport. Not while she rode the transport, at least. Humans rarely pried into a stranger's business. It was safer not to.

But when the transport arrived in Hikeet, officials there would ask questions. Ranita had no embedded info-chip with access codes. She had no signaling device with a digital identification token. She didn't even have a physical ID card, though she could have forged one. Possession of such an outdated commodity would prompt entrance guards to flag her and pull her aside for questioning.

The only device on her person, besides her timepiece, was the tiny beacon, secured around her waist under her tunic. If activated, it would emit a signal on a special frequency and initiate an emergency extraction. But that too, if discovered by the guards, would raise questions she could not answer.

So, she waited. It would have to be a little darker before she could walk alongside the road without being noticed. It would have to be completely dark before she attempted to sneak through the gate or over the wall that surrounded Hikeet without being detected.

She wrapped her arms around her knees and tried to distract herself from her nervous impatience. Tilting her head back, she stared at the tree branches overhead. She had used these trees as cover before without giving them much thought. Now she considered them more carefully.

Their upper branches swayed in the breeze, and the needles rustled and hummed. Their prickly foliage, of a dark glossy green, cast a heavy shade. The air under and around them was laced with the scent of the resin that oozed from the trunks and branches.

Their existence was a wonder. Very few trees survived anywhere near Skakeet City. At one time a bastion of shady avenues and botanical parks, its trees had been blasted or burned during the Great War. In the reorganization that followed the war, Dark Spinners removed most of the remaining trees after discovering their inspiring effect on the human psyche.

Mindful of these few outliers now, Ranita felt their strengthening influence. Her agitation eased, and when the time came to leave her hiding spot, she walked away with a calm, purposeful step. She would save the prisoners or she would not. All she could do was follow the dictates of her training and leave the rest to Ya-Lohim.

The first part of her walk was pleasant. Though some light still filtered through the clouds, she didn't worry about being seen. Anyone who spotted her would assume she was heading for the transport station just over a kilometer ahead, in the direction of Hikeet. By the time she reached the stop, dusk had deepened. If anyone was around, it was too dark for them to notice her and wonder why she avoided the transport.

The rest of the walk was more difficult. There was still enough traffic to make walking on the road unsafe, and there were no walkways here. None were needed. No one ever walked this route. No one except Ranita, forced to stumble over rough, rocky ground in the dark. She almost fell twice. The second stumble occurred perilously near the town wall, close to the gate. She stifled an exclamation and stood still for several minutes afterward, straining for any sound of movement that might indicate she had been heard.

A public transport rumbled toward the gate. It was time to move. If she let this transport pass, she would have to wait for the next one or scale the wall. Neither option suited her.

She darted forward just as the transport's electronic signal triggered the gate's sensors, causing it to swing open. The lead car, where the driver sat, slid by. Crouching as low as possible, Ranita ran close alongside the second car, listening to its whine, her breath held tight and silent so she would hear any variation in the sound that might mean a change of trajectory.

If the transport wobbled even a little, its razor-like protrusions could slice into her, leaving her a bleeding, huddled mass in its wake. Despite this danger, she dared not move away to a safe distance. Sensors on the gate would detect movement in the open space between it and the transport and alert security. The only way to sneak through the gate was to keep close enough to a transport that the sensors couldn't differentiate between its movement and hers.

Ranita kept close to the conveyance for a good twenty meters past the opening. Then she dove and rolled. She executed the maneuver perfectly, coming back to her feet at the bottom of a grassy hill as the transport's lights winked at her in farewell and the gate clicked closed.

She took a deep breath and laughed a shaky laugh, barely audible. Every time she did this, she promised herself she'd scale the wall next time. But that carried its own dangers, and the adrenaline rushing through her veins now was not unwelcome. It provided the energy for a sprint across the wide-open space between the wall and the first buildings. A guard would pass by in the next minute or two and she needed to lose herself in the winding streets before then.

Ranita knew these streets well and made her way, by the most direct route, to the narrow alley behind the Red Peacock Café. An empty crate offered a place to sit, in the deep shadows and out of the way, but still within sight of the café's back door.

Now she must wait again and hope that Rob was working tonight. Most of her other informants in Hikeet were unreliable, sometimes refusing to talk or threatening to turn her in, and much less likely to have useful information. She waited, alternately sweating and unfastening her jacket, and shivering and huddling into its collar. She might be getting too old for this sort of thing.

As soon as the idea surfaced, she dismissed it. Retirement had no appeal for her. Better to die doing this work than to fade into obscurity, useless, sequestered in the hidden home compound, and fretting all the while about what disasters were about to happen on the outside.

A flurry of activity in the alleyway signaled the café's closing time. Staff hauled garbage out to the bins and then began to exit, making their way toward their homes or the nearest transit stop. Ranita left her perch and drew nearer the Red

Peacock, where she could keep close watch on the door. She identified most of the café staff by sight. Cooks. Wait staff. A dishwasher. But not Rob. Sucking in her lower lip, Ranita resisted the urge to yank the door open and charge in to search for him.

The host hadn't come out yet, either. He might have gone out the front, but that would be unusual. Ranita would wait a little longer. She leaned against the building across the way and folded her arms tightly around herself, planting her feet to keep from pacing.

At last, she was rewarded. The host came out, and behind him, Rob's lanky form emerged, unmistakable even in the dim light. He loitered while the host hurried away. Rob's demeanor was furtive, wary, suggesting he was expecting her.

"Rob!" Ranita kept her voice to a loud whisper.

After a quick check around the alleyway, he approached her. "Thought you might come tonight."

She linked her arm with his and nodded toward the near end of the alley. He nodded back, and they sauntered toward the street, heads close together. Anyone who noticed them would believe they saw trysting lovers. Not young lovers. They were both too old to give that impression. But lovers long accustomed to one another. There had been many chances to practice; they made it look natural and comfortable.

Too comfortable, perhaps. Ranita wondered what would happen if she kissed Rob, but she instantly dismissed the idea. Their relationship was perilous enough without added complications. She tugged her thoughts back to her mission.

"What kept you?" she asked. "Everyone else has long since gone home. I about gave up on you."

"Minister of Security decided to show up tonight with a lady friend. Closing time has no meaning for him. We've become his favorite hideaway for clandestine romantic encounters and I, for some unguessed reason, am his favorite waiter. Ironic, isn't it?"

She caught the flash of his sardonic grin and shivered. "His companion? Was she human or Dark Spinner?"

"DS this time. Someone high-ranking, I suspect, and even less worried about closing time than he was."

"Our lives have no meaning for them, do they?" She felt the tension tightening her chest and tried to relax. "Were they spinning?"

He grimaced. "Café got a little spooky toward the end, yes. Think I'd get used to that, but I never have."

"No. It's not natural." She imagined the café's dining room clouded with the twirling, menacing shadows of the Dark Spinners, and her hand tightened on Rob's arm. Just as well she didn't carry a weapon. Murdering Dark Spinners wouldn't bring light to any more people. It would only deepen the darkness.

"I'm guessing you've heard about the raid, if you were expecting me," she said, trying to dispel the images and get back to business. "And the three they took."

"Yes. The young woman's grandfather works at the First Ministry Building. Janitor, or something like. He's quite distraught."

"Have you spoken to him?"

"No. Just got word through communication lines. I doubt there's much he can do to help them, but he should know where they're being held. Might know something about the movements of workers and guards in the holding area."

"Where can I find him?"

"He's working night shift. I sent word someone would meet him in the morning when his shift is done. There's a little sculpture garden on the north side of the First Ministry Building. Usually deserted. Do you know it?"

"Yes. Isn't there some way I can get to him sooner? It's too risky to try to infiltrate during the day. If I can't formulate a plan in the next hour or two, I'll have to wait until tomorrow night. But that's risky, too. Lives are at stake if they talk."

He shrugged, then pulled her closer and leaned his head down, brushing her hair with his cheek. "Don't worry. The Ministry won't realize there's any reason to hurry. Word is the current inquisitor likes to make people wait and squirm for a while before he starts on them. And then he takes it slow. Seems to relish his job. Doesn't want it to be over too soon."

Now Rob shuddered and Ranita could felt the tension in his arm linked through hers.

"We never seem to make any progress." Ranita tasted bitterness on her tongue. "Is anything we're doing here worth the risk?"

After a long moment of silence, Rob answered, his voice coming slow and hesitant. "We'll never change the spinners. As a species, they're scum, filled with corruption and evil. You and I have agreed on that for a long time. But you're saving some of our people. I'd like to think I'm helping with that. And each one counts. Besides . . ."

He paused and pulled his arm out of their link, slipping it around her waist and snugging her tight against his side. "I hope you never stop. How else would I ever get to see you? These trysts are the highlights of my life. If you give up, I'll have to figure out another way to meet up."

He reached for her shoulder with his free hand, rotating her so that she pressed up against his chest. He leaned down and placed a lingering kiss on her lips. For a moment she gave way, let her own lips respond. This was what she had wanted for a long time. Then she pushed him away.

"An interesting idea," she murmured, "but I can't get distracted. Too much is at stake."

He sighed. "Can't let the scum win. Not this time."

3

THE OLD JANITOR

Without speaking further, they linked arms again and continued along the street. Before they reached the transit station, they parted without speaking. Rob entered the queue for the next transit back to Skakeet City, and Ranita melted into the shadow of the station building. She watched Rob for a moment, noticing the endearing awkwardness of his lanky form and letting herself love him, just for a moment.

She took a room at a seedy inn in the poorer part of town. Its usual clients were disreputable. A few of them were probably doing things with Dark Spinners she didn't want to know about. But the proprietor knew her and let her slip in and out without calling attention to her presence. He gave her a room at the end of the hall near the back door and accepted her cash tokens without asking for digital registration. His only requirement of her was that she be gone before the rest of the guests began to circulate in the morning.

She watched the sun come up from the deserted sculpture garden, just beyond the shadowy bulk of the First Ministry Building. She breathed deeply in the fresh morning air. Hikeet, for all its urban sophistication, had the smell of the country. Not surprising. The ruling Dark Spinners would never put up with the bad, industrial air, nearly unbreathable, that residents of Skakeet City were forced to live with.

They couldn't be bothered to train technologists to keep the air scrubbers working in industrial areas, and they expected the power to keep coming, to keep running their conveniences, but they saw no reason to subject themselves to the negative consequences of their demands. Ranita balled her hands into fists and kept her gaze away from the grand houses down the avenue from the garden, reflecting again on how fortunate it was that she didn't carry a weapon.

The early sunshine bathed the marble and granite figures with soft, warm hues of rose and yellow. She crouched in the shadow of a massive obelisk and waited for the light to breathe lifelikeness into the statues, marveling at their existence as she had done with the trees the evening before. A relic of a time before Dark Spinners ruled, the garden had somehow been overlooked when they took over this suburb of Skakeet City. If it ever came to their attention, the sculptures would be pulverized, making way for something dark and modern.

Ranita had done a thorough check of the garden upon arrival, but now she double-checked around each of the sculptures and then walked the entire perimeter. She wished, not for the first time in her career, that she had the ability to detect the auras of Dark Spinners, as they could do with each other. At least they could not sense humans, so they wouldn't have that advantage over her. Feeling as secure as was possible and checking her escape routes, she chose a spot that concealed her while giving her a view of all the entrances.

The old janitor arrived a few minutes later. He pretended to study the marble fountain, dry now, topped with an ornate carving of a powerful figure with sword held aloft. A Light Immortal, Ranita suspected. No mortal had such a noble face and confident bearing.

She approached the old man. He started when he saw her, but held his ground.

"You're Bella's grandfather?" Ranita asked softly.

"Yes. Are you here to help her?"

"If I can. I need to know anything you can tell me about where she's being held, the guards' rotations in that area, the entrance codes. And anything else you can think of."

"Whatever information I could get is here." He laid a small disk on the edge of the fountain. "They're in the lowest level. I couldn't get down there to see them, to see if they're all right." He reached out to grasp the edge of the fountain, turning away from Ranita. "But they're not all right. How could they be? They're in the lowest level, you know. Interrogation five, I heard someone say. I was down there once. To clean up after a messy session." He shuddered, though his voice remained level, without emotion.

Ranita waited for him to say more, but the old man remained silent. She prodded him back to speech. "What room are they in?"

"What? The room? I don't know. There are only four rooms. If you can get down there, you can find them."

"That area's controlled by digital access codes, yes?"

"Yes." He angled his head toward her, keeping his body slanted away. He scrunched his face into a frown, as if he expected her next question.

"And are the codes included on your disk?"

"No. Not those. Everything else, though."

"Can you get them for me?"

"No. Only Dark Spinners have those."

"I'll need the codes. You'll have to get them for me before nightfall."

He turned to face her squarely, his face darkened by a frown. "I'm just a janitor. How would I get the codes?"

"I don't know, but your granddaughter's life, along with the lives of the others, depends on it."

He looked away from her, staring at the First Ministry Building as he spoke. "I'll do anything else I can to help you. Maybe create a distraction for you. Or even go down with you. But the codes? You'll have to find a Dark Spinner for those. Some of them might help you if you threaten them. Hold them at knife point. Shoot them. Something. I don't know. Or skip the codes and blast your way in. The locks aren't that strong. It wouldn't take much more than a laser pistol."

Ranita balled her hands into fists as she stifled an angry retort. She had no weapon. And what weapon would hold a Dark Spinner, anyway? They would simply spin into shadow and wisp away. The likelihood of coercing a Dark Spinner to give her the codes was zero. Worse yet, was the idea of blasting her way into the building. Her rescue would be short-lived indeed if she tried that. The old janitor would have to come up with a way to get the codes.

Ranita took a step toward him. He backed away from her. She moved to the side of the fountain, tapped the disk he had placed there with one finger. "What you suggest is impossible. But you understand the ways of the Ministry. You'll figure out how. To get the codes, I mean."

His gaze darted back toward her. "Knowing about the Ministry won't help me any. I'm still just human." He paused. "Unless . . ." His eyes shifted away from her face again.

"Unless? You do know a way, then."

"I might know someone. It would be dangerous. I can't promise anything."

"Make it work. How long will it take? When can I meet you again?"

"Come here before my shift tonight. Two hours before change of watch. I'll meet you or send someone. But I'm not promising, remember? I suggest you bring your weapons and be ready to use them. I have to go now, before someone sees me talking to you."

He scurried away, weaving his way from one statue to the next until he reached the street. He peered around, stepped out, and marched away, heading toward a nearby transit stop.

As Ranita watched him go, a great weariness descended over her. She palmed the disk and secreted it in a trouser pocket, knowing it was a futile gesture. She sighed, a deep, loud sigh. She wasn't going to win this time. The chances the janitor would get the codes were slim to none. And there was no way to break the prisoners free from the lowest level without access codes, no other plan she could make that would have any chance of success.

She would fail, and the prisoners would talk. Sooner or later, they would be unable to endure the torture of the interrogators, and they would talk. The resistance groups in the city would be compromised. Worse than that, depending on how much the prisoners knew, Ranita's own small community, far from here and hidden both by superior technology and by cunning, would be at risk.

A hint of movement from the far side of the obelisk caught Ranita's eye, and she stiffened. Was someone there? She knew no one had been there when she arrived, but the old man had distracted her, and she had forgotten to watch for a wisp of shadow on the air, a swirl of darkness that might be the only sign of a Dark Spinner's arrival. She made a quick assessment of the surrounding sculptures, trying to plan the best escape route. But she knew it was too late for that a moment later, when a Dark Spinner woman walked around from the back side of the obelisk.

4

—·—

AN ASTONISHING PROPOSAL

Heat flooded Ranita's body and her breathing accelerated, preparing her for flight, though fleeing was no longer a possibility. The Dark Spinner held the beginnings of a spin; it would only take a small shift for her to translate to a full spin. If Ranita tried to run now, she'd be enveloped in shadow before she reached the street. She pushed hard against the flight response and studied this Dark Spinner instead, alert for any sign of a weakness she could exploit.

The Dark Spinner was around twenty-five or thirty—young by the standards of her long-lived species. She was even taller than the average spinner; Ranita, though tall for a human, had to tilt her head up to meet the woman's eyes. And those eyes. Brilliant emerald green, with flecks of dazzling gold to match the shimmer of golden hair. Ranita felt a surge of admiration, even as her limbs shook with the twin urges to attack or run, and with the effort to restrain those urges.

The two of them stood assessing one another with narrowed eyes for moments that stretched into eternity. The Dark Spinner was the first to move. She shifted, then backed up to lean against the obelisk and crossed her arms. She let a hint of a smile play across her lips.

"Well, now. Planning a prison break, it seems. Unless my ears betray me."

"Not everything one overhears is what it seems," Ranita answered, wondering how much the spinner had heard.

"That's true. But I think there's no mistake this time."

"What are you going to do?" Might as well get to the bad news right away.

"That depends entirely on you."

"Explain."

"You might be able to procure something I want, and in exchange, I can provide something you need."

Ranita's breathing eased and steadied. She couldn't imagine what she could get that this Dark Spinner would want, but engaging in negotiations might give her the wiggle room she needed to escape.

"What do I need that you can provide?"

The Spinner shrugged. "Well, let's see. I heard something about codes a few minutes ago. I've got connections you can't even imagine. No need for you to knife or laser one of my people to coerce them into spilling classified information. If we can come to an agreement, at any rate."

"Codes?" Ranita's disbelief tinged her voice. This Dark Spinner, one of the scum of society and, therefore, inherently untrustworthy, was offering to help her break subversive humans out of high security detention? "Codes won't come cheap, I'm guessing. What would you want in return? And aren't you taking a huge risk talking to me like this? Unless this is a set-up. If any other Dark Spinners are around, you'll go down with me."

The woman tossed her golden hair with a smirk. "There are no Dark Spinner auras within several hundred meters. The nearest are in the First Ministry Building, and unconcerned with me. As for what I want in return for those costly codes . . ."

Ranita shook her head. This was beyond her experience, surreal. She saw tension seep into the Dark Spinner's graceful form. She took a step forward, letting her hand rest on the edge of the fountain, borrowing strength from the statue of the Immortal towering over her. "Yes? What can you possibly want?"

The Spinner unfolded her arms and held out her hands. Shadow encased them. Ranita shuddered and was about to turn away when a flicker of color caught her eye, a swirling of red flecks in the shadow, like the color flecks in a spinner's eyes.

The red brightened, took on a range of hues. Orange mixed with the reds and bled into amber. The colors were absorbing the shadow, gaining ground. Blues and greens fought now for a place in the churning sheath that wrapped itself around the Spinner's hands, becoming brighter and brighter. Ranita, staring in disbelief, saw, for the briefest moment, a spark of white light weaving its way through the brilliant hues, but before she could be certain, it winked out.

The spinner kept her eyes on her hands a little longer before dropping them with a shrug. All hint of the spin dissipated. She held herself still for a long moment, then lifted her face and met Ranita's gaze.

"I can't spin pure light," she said.

"Would you want to?" Ranita didn't try to keep the heavy doubt out of her voice.

"Not every Dark Spinner wants to be one. I was born here. My family all spins shadow. And my friends. It's how I was trained, and I entered professional life based on that training. No one ever gave me a choice. No one even considered I might prefer to spin light. It just isn't done. But it's what I want, more than anything." She straightened and her gaze became direct, hard. "And if you ever reveal that to anyone, I'll turn you in as a dissenter and make sure you meet the head inquisitor."

She couldn't be sincere. There was a hidden agenda here somewhere, but until Ranita figured out what it was, she needed to play along. "I won't give you away. But I don't understand how you think I can help you. I'm human. I don't know the first thing about spinning, light or dark. You'll need to find someone else to teach you."

"Yes. But if there's anyone on Exalton that can, they keep themselves well hidden, and for good reason. Even if I knew what to do, I'm too well-known and visible to do it without serious repercussions. My only chance is to leave Exalton. Get to Luxera somehow."

"That makes sense," Ranita agreed, speaking slowly, trying to think through a correct response. "But again, I can't help you. I don't have the capability of transporting you or anyone else off-world. Why don't you just spin away? Your people do it all the time."

"No. Not really. Only trained subversion agents spin away, when they're given a mission or an off-world assignment. I'm an artist. I'm not eligible for off-world training, and without that training, I have no way to acquire the coordinates for other worlds. No coordinates, no spinning away. Just like, no codes, no prisoner rescue." She raised her eyebrows as if to ask whether Ranita understood her.

For the first time, Ranita almost believed this encounter was happening. It made sense, in a way that skewed her perceptions of Dark Spinners. She still didn't trust this woman, but she saw a way to make this work for her. At the very least, it might provide an escape from the garden.

"I don't have the coordinates," she said. "They weren't included in my training either."

"But you can get them."

"Maybe. It will take some time." Ranita did a quick estimate. "Five or six hours, minimum. Possibly more."

"Then you'd best get to it. Where will you meet me, and when?"

Ideas, wild thoughts tumbled through Ranita's brain. She tried to marshal them into order and make sense of them. She would need help to procure the coordinates, which meant leaving Hikeet.

"Where?" the woman asked again. "Back here? You have to meet the old man, after all."

"No. Not here. Not in Hikeet. There's a village about eight kilometers south of town. Evergreen is its name. Meet me outside the wall, by the east gate, just before dusk."

The woman nodded. "Evergreen, I know. But just before dusk is a little vague."

"You'll figure it out. Don't be late. I have work to do afterward, provided you keep your end of the bargain."

"Ah, yes. Your little prison break. Very well. Just before dusk, it is. I'll be there. Make sure you are too."

5

— · —

GILAD'S ANSWER

The Dark Spinner's physical form lost its cohesion as she swirled into shadow and darted away. Watching the transition left Ranita with a queasy stomach, but she had no time to indulge in her revulsion. Her hand slipped under her tunic and found the beacon secreted there. Activation required only slight pressure on its smooth button. Gilad would receive the signal and come find her.

He should be in or near Skakeet City today, but it still might take time for him to get to her, depending on what covert activities he was involved in. She could help him by moving to a location better suited for extraction. Moving through Hikeet with the ease of long familiarity, she choose side streets and back alleys, but headed always toward the south wall. She knew a place where a grassy hillock created a spot to scale the wall more easily. It was risky to go over in daylight, but time was short, and a tall office building nearby would create enough shade to make her less conspicuous.

But before she reached the hillock, she heard a low whine nearby. Gilad had already found her. The sound was so faint that an untrained ear would never have picked it out from among the city sounds. But she had ridden in Gilad's cloaked skimmer before and knew its tonal signature. Besides, the beacon under her tunic vibrated against her skin, letting her know Gilad had seen her.

She made a quick survey of the area, as Gilad would also be doing. There was no one in sight, human or spinner. A flicker in the landscape caught her eye, and the next moment, Gilad's skimmer popped into view. A haphazard-looking vehicle, it had side plates of various metals and colors, and a hint of rust, carefully applied, which presented no danger to the skimmer's structural integrity. The body appeared old and worthless, but it concealed some of the most advanced technology in the world.

The passenger door slid open, spilling out a cascade of organ notes, hastily muted as Ranita slipped into the seat. As soon as the door closed, Gilad punched a button and the cloak's indicator light brightened. Safety belts snugged over Ranita's shoulders as the vehicle lifted smoothly off the ground. In a moment, they were over the wall and shooting out into the countryside.

Ranita expelled her breath and shot a glance at Gilad. Dark-haired, dark-eyed, olive-complected, he radiated intensity until he turned his gaze toward her and grinned. He ran his finger over the controls for the sound system, and the rumble of organ notes rose to a loud whisper.

"Haven't had to rescue you in a while," he said, and his grin grew wider.

He was in a light-hearted mood, not upset by being called away from his own work. Good. Might make it easier for him to deal with the request she was about to make of him.

She gave him a tentative smile. "I'm afraid I need more than a simple rescue this time."

"It will cost you, whatever it is."

"Everything does, it seems. Sometimes more than I can pay."

His grin faded. "You're serious, aren't you? I just meant your famous nut pastries. But you know I'll help you however I can. What do you need?"

How to start? She shook her head, searching for the right words. "Would you believe a Dark Spinner if she told you she wants to spin light?"

"Huh? Well." He paused to manipulate the skimmer's controls, but his puzzled frown suggested he was stalling, trying to formulate an answer. "Hmm. I guess it would depend on the circumstances. If the old chronicles are accurate, they're all descended from the Luxerans, the Light Spinners. Maybe spinning light is their natural default, unless they're taught otherwise. So, yes, I suppose it's possible."

"I don't agree. I think they're totally corrupt. They can't, or at least they won't, change. And yet, it's my only chance to help the dissenters escape custody."

Gilad stared at her. "This is a real thing, isn't it? Tell me."

She related the whole story, describing in detail the Dark Spinner and her attempt, almost successful, to spin pure light.

"And so, I need you to get Luxera's coordinates for me if you can. If you will. Knowing that I'll give them to a Dark Spinner who is totally untrustworthy. I doubt she'll give me the codes, even if she can get them. She'll probably turn me in, and they'll torture me until I betray everything and everyone I love. Even the tiny spark of light that exists on this world will be snuffed out."

Gilad brought the skimmer down, landing well out in the countryside, where the walls of Hikeet were visible only as a thin line and Skakeet City was a smudge of smog on the horizon. Even the closest settlement, the village of Evergreen, was too far away for anyone there to spot the skimmer. Gilad turned off the cloak and opened the windows, letting in fresh air and the sound of birdsong. Then he sat without speaking for a long time. Ranita wanted to press him, to get him to agree to her request, or to tell her she was foolish to even consider giving the Dark Spinner the coordinates. But she held her tongue. Thoughtful and wise for so young a man, Gilad would take his time to come to a conclusion. The right conclusion.

At last, he turned to her, and she saw a smile lurking in the corners of his mouth, though his eyes were sober.

"I've never thought about the choices the Dark Spinners do or don't have. But it makes sense. People who repress others would be likely to repress their own kind as well, though in a more subtle way. Social pressure can be hard to resist. But some of them might want to. This Dark Spinner must have a lot of courage, or want desperately to spin light, or both, to speak to you so openly."

Ranita's mouth fell open. "You believe she's sincere?"

Gilad shrugged. "Hard to tell from where I sit. I haven't spoken with her. But I believe she could be. Otherwise, why didn't she apprehend you right away? And if she is, she deserves a choice as much as we do." He smiled wryly, with a shake of his head. "I've always believed our mission is to bring Ya-Lohim's light to the humans on our world who are oppressed by darkness. But why shouldn't we bring light to Dark Spinners as well?"

He fell silent for a moment, then inclined his head toward Ranita. "You have the final call, of course. You're the one who has to figure out what to do with whatever information she brings. You're the one who will be risking your life to free the prisoners. What do you want me to do?"

Ranita took a deep breath. This wasn't what she had expected. She had figured she was foolish for even considering working with a Dark Spinner and had been prepared for Gilad to tell her so. And yet, at his words, her stomach, which she hadn't even realized was queasy, settled and unknotted.

"Well, then." She took another deep breath. "I need the coordinates for Luxera by dusk. Can you get them?"

"I can try. It might take a little looking unless Abraham has come across them and catalogued them. Where shall I meet you? Where are you meeting your Dark Spinner?"

Not *my* Dark Spinner! she wanted to shout at him. But instead, she answered in a matter-of-fact tone. "Just outside the east gate of Evergreen. Right before dusk."

"Evergreen?" He raised his eyebrows. "Where so many of our supporters live? Where dissent and insurrection flourish? You must trust this person more than you realize."

"I don't," she answered quickly. "I don't trust her at all. How could I? I didn't think about all the vulnerable people I'm leading her to. I must be losing my edge. I just tried to think of a place that's familiar to me, and with all that open land there, I can scan for other spinners coming with her or following her. It's the best I could come up with on short notice."

His grin flashed out again. "It will do fine. I need to get going. You haven't given me a lot of time. Where do you want me to drop you? Or are you coming with me?"

"I have some research to do. You can let me out here and I'll walk to Evergreen."

He touched his control panel and Ranita's door opened. She stepped out and patted her pocket, reassuring herself that the janitor's disk was still secure, then nodded to Gilad. As the door slid shut, she heard the organ music increase in volume. The skimmer accelerated, then shimmered and disappeared, cloaked again. The soft whine of its engines faded as she started walking.

6

— · —

SUSPSICIOUS DATA

Ranita kept a sharp eye on her surroundings as she headed toward Evergreen, looking for any suspicious activity or signs of Dark Spinners. The village lay in a wide swath of pastureland. A grove of trees wrapped around its north and west sides, nestling close against its walls, but there was no other cover, nothing to hide Ranita's approach. It made her vulnerable, but it would also make it harder for Dark Spinners to get close without being seen.

About a ten-minute walk east of the village, the ruins of an older, larger town lay strewn across the grassland. The structures, what little remained of them, were of stone or brick from a time before modern building materials had come into use. The only walls more than waist high were those of the ancient cathedral, built of stone and constructed to outlast all but the most destructive forces. It was one of the stray remainders of an earlier time, somehow escaping the notice of the Dark Spinners. The walls themselves, and the dome that towered over them, were not the greatest wonders preserved here. A relic of a time when worship of Ya-Lohim was formalized and regular, the cathedral harbored a large and intricate pipe organ.

Gilad had discovered it in pieces, many of its pipes serving as homes for the small animals that had moved in after the people moved out. With a determination beyond Ranita's comprehension, he had labored for nearly a year, whenever he had time, to restore the instrument. But when he had it in working order at last, he played it for her, and she understood his love, his desire.

She shivered now, at the memory of the sound, glorious beyond her wildest expectations. Perhaps he would stay late this evening and play after they concluded the business with the Dark Spinner. She would not have time to linger and listen if he did.

Ranita spent the afternoon in the back room of a small café in Evergreen. The proprietor, though not part of the local resistance group, was a sympathizer, and Ranita often frequented his establishment. He had become her ally and her friend.

She borrowed a disk reader from him and pored over the information the janitor had provided, understanding it and memorizing it. The old man had been thorough with his rundown of guard assignments, patrol routines, feeding schedules, and other details of life in the First Ministry high-security holding area. And all this on short notice.

Was his attention to detail driven by his concern for his granddaughter? Or was he part of a setup? Perhaps even the prisoners were part of a plot to draw Ranita and other operatives from her secret community in. The ruling authorities had occasionally captured someone from the larger resistance movement, but never an operative from the home complex, someone who could reveal its hidden location.

The Dark Spinners had been aware of the community's existence since the war. At the war's end, the Immortals had spirited the Sashosa, the world's other species, to a new world. Most of the humans still loyal to Ya-Lohim, calling themselves the Wellador, followed in their void ships.

These were the exiles Ranita and her fellow agents looked for when they turned their eyes to the sky. The exiles whose promise to return engendered both hope and despair.

But a remnant of the Welador, Ranita's own ancestors, had stayed behind, determined to bring light and healing to Exalton. They worked carefully, using both their cunning and their advanced technology to remain hidden. It took all their resources, and the Dark Spinners were always just a breath away from discovering their location.

Ranita usually kept two steps ahead of them, laughing at their blunders as they stumbled along behind, trying to decipher the clues and deliberate misdirection she left in her wake. What spooked her so much this time that she saw conspiracies where, most likely, none existed? Was she overcompensating for her failure to anticipate the ambush that had forced her to ditch her skimmer in the sea? If so, she needed to sharpen up. Or retire.

She shook her head and bent over the disk reader again. She knew why she was having a hard time trusting the old janitor's data. A Dark Spinner had upended the mission, raising questions about everything Ranita thought she knew. And Dark Spinners were by nature deceitful. Now, asked to trust one, she wasn't sure she could do it. Questioning that, she questioned everything, the janitor included.

And yet, the operation was in motion. To stop it now would be almost as risky as going through with it. The Dark Spinner would come in a few hours, and Ranita would meet her at the boundary between daylight and shadow.

She looked up, seeking the reassurance of sunlight. The room had only one tiny window, but it let in a slanted ray of pure, warm light. Ranita nodded with a slight smile. Such a small beam, but it was enough. She turned back to her perusal of the janitor's disk.

When the sun began to dip toward the west, she ordered some food from the café's simple menu and fortified herself for the evening's work. As soon as she finished her meal, she slipped out the west gate and into the small grove of trees that leaned close against the town walls. She edged along the west wall, turned, and continued along the north wall until the trees thinned, stepping carefully to avoid snapping branches underfoot. Then she tried out several spots, looking for a place that afforded a good view of the land in front of the east gate and also to the north, toward Hikeet. A vantage point from which to see the Dark Spinner coming before the Dark Spinner saw her.

With more than an hour until dusk, she made herself comfortable, sitting with her back against a tree and her legs stretched out before her, and prepared to wait. Again. This past day had been filled with too much waiting. She tried not to fret about what the inquisitor might have learned from the prisoners, or what he might yet learn this evening before she could make a rescue attempt.

Fretting did no good and wore at her focus. Struggling to school her thoughts, she tried one of her favorite tricks to get her mind off worry. Letting her gaze rove across the landscape, she listened intently, trying to pick out insect noises and identify individual bird songs.

But it wasn't birdsong that came to her, nor yet the buzz of insects or the rustle of the wind in the trees. Instead, she heard the unmistakable tones of organ music—long, drawn out, beautifully modulating chords followed by the faster moving phrases of a fugue. Her eyes darted to the cathedral. There was no sign of Gilad's skimmer, but Ranita had no doubt it was there, somewhere, still cloaked or hidden from sight on the far side of the structure.

He was back earlier than expected. That could only mean he had found the coordinates. He would not have given up so quickly if he had been unable to find them. But what a risk he took, playing the organ such a short time before the appointment with the Dark Spinner.

Ranita stood and crept closer to the last trees, checking the level of remaining daylight. There was still a little time. Gilad would stop playing soon and come find her. He had to. She needed the coordinates in hand ahead of time.

But the music continued. Ranita shifted from one foot to the other, taking deep breaths, trying to squelch the urge to run across the pasture to the cathedral and confront Gilad. She wouldn't see the Dark Spinner arrive if she did that.

She peered toward Hikeet, and then her heart skipped a beat, pounded madly, and skipped another beat. With still more than half an hour until dusk, a tendril of shadow already wended its way across the landscape. Was this her golden-haired Dark Spinner or some other DS heading in this direction on a different errand?

The shadow came on fast, heading, not for the east gate, but for the grove of trees where Ranita stood. She slunk back into the thick of the grove, closer to the town wall, and watched, holding her breath. The shadow hovered over a spot near where Ranita had been standing just a moment before, and then the swirling darkness began to take on solid form.

Keeping still and silent, Ranita observed, fascinated, as the Dark Spinner's body took shape. The hair glinted in the late afternoon sunlight, leaving no doubt that this was the same woman she had spoken to this morning. Even before the last of the shadows dissipated, the woman assumed a watchful posture and gazed out toward the east gate. There was no one in sight near the gate, and the woman's head swiveled as she checked the whole sweep of the pastureland.

She stiffened and leaned her head forward in the direction of the cathedral as the strains of organ music swelled. Ranita stifled an exclamation of dismay when the woman swirled into shadow again and darted across the space between Evergreen and the ruins. As soon as she vacated the grove of trees, Ranita scurried forward to monitor her movement.

The Dark Spinner coalesced again just outside the cathedral entrance. Her shape was barely discernible from this distance, and yet Ranita could see, in the lean of the shape, that the DS had assumed a posture of listening.

7

FUGUE

Ranita, also listening, heard the music take on the deep tones of the organ's lower registers. What was Gilad thinking? Even from this distance, Ranita felt the reverberations on the air. The DS woman must be vibrating along with them, as close as she was.

And then she stepped up to the cathedral and disappeared inside. Ranita stood frozen, waiting for the music to stop, expecting the sounds of confrontation, fearing to see Gilad hauled off in the swirling embrace of a dark spin to share the prison cell of the three dissenters Ranita had hoped to rescue.

What should she do? Try to help Gilad? Or would it be better to get back to Skakeet City and her own skimmer? If she headed for home immediately, she could warn the community. They would need time to prepare for the possibility that Gilad would break under the inquisitor's hand.

Not sure what to do, her body decided for her. She found herself sprinting across the uneven ground, catching her breath as she stumbled over rocky places, and then surging forward again. What would have been a ten-minute walk felt like a run that would never end, but finally she halted, panting, outside the cathedral doors. They stood ajar, and the music poured out of them, filling Ranita's senses and making rational thought difficult.

Her lungs filled with air, and the instinct of long training took over. There was no need to plan a strategy now, only the need to be alert, prepared to react to whatever she found inside. Taking one last deep breath, she stepped through the doors and into the dim interior.

An artificial torch perched on the organ console's music rack, illuminating the keys and Gilad's hands. Those hands moved with skill and grace, and Gilad's body bobbed and swayed as his feet reached for the pedals. Ranita glimpsed his face in the mirrors angled along the top of the console. His expression revealed his complete absorption in the music. Was he aware of the Dark Spinner's presence?

The Dark Spinner stood about two-thirds of the way up the center aisle of the nave. She cocked her head to one side, her face toward the organ. Ranita saw no sign of any spun shadow swirling about her person, though in such dim light it was hard to be sure. Ranita stood at the back end of the aisle, as motionless as the DS woman, ready for any action.

As if time had stopped, the two women remained still while the music filled them, building, swelling, modulating and building again, until, at last, it rose to its final resolution. Ranita felt its vibrations through the floor, through her fingers, thrilling through her core, as if bolts of raw energy jolted through her. The music modulated again, decreasing in volume, dying away. A few last notes fell on her ear, soft tones that echoed the resolution, and the pipes were stilled.

The last echoes faded and in their aftermath a silence greater and more profound than the music itself filled the space. Gilad sat without moving while Ranita's heart slowed and took on a regular rhythm. Then, in a motion that caused both women to start, he rotated on the bench to face out toward the nave.

"What do you think? Did you like the music?" He focused his gaze on the Dark Spinner and his voice was calm, unsurprised. So, he had been aware of her while he played.

"I've never experienced anything like that before," the woman answered. "It was marvelous. What is this place? What is that . . . instrument?"

Gilad threw his arms out, taking in the expanse of the spacious building. "This is the Cathedral of Jerome's Star. A place of worship once, but almost as well known, in its day, as a stellar observatory. And this instrument is a pipe organ. Once, Exalton was blessed with more than a hundred such cathedrals with pipe organs, some much larger than this one, but most are in ruins now, or have completely disappeared. To my knowledge, this is the only working pipe organ in the world today. You've just witnessed a bit of our history come alive."

The woman considered for a moment. "So, such music was once common. And are there others who can still play as you do?"

"Not that I'm aware of. How would they learn? Where would they practice? And what would happen to them when the authorities discovered them?" Gilad's voice held an unmistakable challenge for the Dark Spinner. What was she going to do with the knowledge he had handed her?

Ranita shrank back into the shadows, her heart thumping as she waited for the answer. She didn't understand why Gilad was opening himself to such risk, offering himself as a sacrifice to this woman of darkness. If the DS chose to take him into custody, he would be hard pressed to evade her. He must know this. He had seen Dark Spinners translate to shadow as often as Ranita had. He knew the startling speed of such transitions.

If this concerned him, he gave no sign of it.

The Dark Spinner laughed. Her laughter held a sharp edge that sent an extra shot of adrenaline racing through Ranita's veins.

"The authorities would come," the woman said, biting off each word, "and the musician would be defenseless. Light might hold them off if you generated the right sort and of adequate strength, but I doubt you could manage it." Her gaze shifted meaningfully to the torch behind Gilad's shoulder and then back to his face. "A flash of light in the eyes might give you a running start, but I doubt it would do much good in the end. They would demolish the organ and incarcerate anyone attempting to play it on charges of unsanctioned cultural activity. But I think you know all this, and yet you play openly. You don't realize, perhaps, who you are playing for."

"No, you're wrong." Gilad's voice was soft, like the echo of the pipes as the last chord died away. "I glimpsed your face while I was playing. Whatever your status, whatever your authority, you are not of the kind you described. I don't believe you would want the organ demolished, nor the organist detained. You hear in the music the same light you long to spin."

"What do you know of what I long to do?"

"Only what Nita has told me. Only what I read in your face."

"Nita?" The Dark Spinner's voice took on a guarded note.

"My friend. You spoke to her this morning. Suggested an exchange of information to your mutual benefit."

"Did she tell you that? She's taken some unexpected liberties, but I wouldn't believe everything she says."

Gilad laughed softly. "Trust me, I don't. That's why I'm here. I needed to see and hear for myself. But if you're worried about Nita's trustworthiness, be assured. The only reason she spoke to me is that she was short on time and needed help to procure the information."

"And you're that help? Do you have what I asked for?" The hunger in the Dark Spinner's voice was palpable. She leaned forward, then stopped and pulled back abruptly. Watching her from behind, Ranita saw the shoulders snap as the woman stiffened her spine.

"Yes," Gilad answered. "Do you have what Nita needs?"

"Maybe. But I'm supposed to meet her by the town walls. If she kept her word, she'll be waiting for me now. What will she do, who will she tell, if I'm not there?"

"Nothing. No one. Because she's not there either. Nita, come forward so our friend can see you."

Gilad gestured in Ranita's direction, and the Dark Spinner turned with an audible gasp. She muttered, her voice too low for Ranita to catch any words, but they sounded like a curse. Ranita stepped forward.

A broken segment of the cathedral's dome left the center aisle of the nave open to the sky. The light of day was spent, but the gleam of a crescent moon filtered down. Augmenting the glow of Gilad's torch, it provided enough illumination for the two women to watch each other's movements, though not enough to delineate facial features.

Gilad reached back to grab the torch from the organ console and brought it toward the women, until the three of them stood uneasily in its light. For a long moment, no one moved or spoke. Ranita wasn't sure what to say. The wrong word might send this Dark Spinner hurtling away without delivering the codes. Or worse, it might send her off to fetch the authorities back to this unsanctioned cultural site.

Finally, the Dark Spinner tossed her head. Her hair caught and scattered flecks of light. "This isn't working. Isn't going to work. I should have known better. I won't hand over sensitive information without assurances, which I doubt you're prepared to give." She took a step toward the cathedral entrance.

"Wait," Gilad said. "We're at your mercy. We need your help. What assurances do you want?"

"I need the coordinates first. And some way to verify that they're more than a random jumble of numbers."

"Of course. Can you memorize them, or should I give you a reader chip? Memorizing would be better, for your own security."

"I can memorize them. You're not going to make me hand over the codes first?"

"No."

Ranita clenched her hands into fists and leaned from her heels onto the balls of her feet. Gilad was giving in too easily. They were going to get played.

What would happen if she jumped the Dark Spinner and threw her to the ground before she could start spinning? Would the woman turn into shadow and mist under her hands, or would the unexpected attack be disconcerting enough to hold her to her physical form?

That was something Ranita had never tried. The only force she had ever brought to bear against a Dark Spinner had been from the right end of a laser pistol. A Dark Spinner struck with a laser blast bled and died just like a human. They seemed ephemeral wisps of shadow, yet they were solid flesh at death, their blood splattering, pooling, and staining their clothing a deep rust red, a deep, mortal red.

Ranita trembled as the memory of spurting blood with its strong, bitter scent blurred her vision and burned her nostrils. Blinking hard, she opened her fists and leaned back on her heels, trying to recapture the threads of the conversation. She carried no weapon, and this Dark Spinner was not a threat. Not yet.

"You're foolish," the Dark Spinner told Gilad. "Makes me wonder if I can trust your data. If the coordinates were real, you'd be more reluctant to give them over."

Gilad chuckled. "You won't trust me if I don't give you the coordinates, but if I do, then I'm too eager and you won't trust me, anyway. You're right. This doesn't seem to be working." He leaned forward and pitched his voice lower, his whole being taking on a subtle intensity. "Nita would drive a hard bargain with you. But I saw your face during the music. It glowed. You're moving toward light. You're not going to be able to restrain yourself, and I'm guessing that will get you into a world of trouble."

Gilad let a space of silence fall between them. The Dark Spinner was tense, her body angled toward the door. But she didn't move. She stood poised, as if between the trouble that would find her if she was discovered consorting with humans and the trouble that would find her if she was discovered spinning light she could not control. Her gaze remained fastened on Gilad, waiting.

He smiled. "You might not believe this, but I want to help you. I'll give you the coordinates, regardless of what you decide about the codes. You can check them with any reasonably powerful telescope. Luxera will be visible, though you can't detect it with the naked eye. There's a suitable lens at the university in Skakeet City. I imagine you can get access to it. Are you ready? Here they are."

He rattled off a set of numbers, followed by a short list of instructions, including several sets of intermediary coordinates. Ranita cringed at the sound of her planned rescue slipping away as he gave away her bargaining advantage. But there was no stopping him now. He repeated everything, then asked the Dark Spinner, "Have you got that? Say it all back to me."

She repeated the numbers and directions he had given her, her voice softer, faltering once as she tried to remember it all.

"Again." Gilad's voice was demanding. He made her repeat the directions two more times, until she said them without stumbling. Then he stepped back and gave her a quick nod. "I hope that helps you find what you seek."

"And the codes?"

"That's up to you. If you trust what I've given you, keep your bargain with Nita and deliver what you promised. Only you can decide if our side of the bargain has been kept to your satisfaction."

8

—·—

WHOM TO TRUST?

The Dark Spinner studied Gilad's face, then nodded. "I have a chip here. It's clandestine technology, so you won't be able to trace it back to me. I've coded it to self-destruct. You'll have about an hour, so don't delay in getting what you need from it." She glanced at Ranita, including her in the warning. "If you get caught, don't expect me to help you, or to give any indication I've ever seen you before. If you suggest to the interrogator that I'm involved with you, I have the means to make you regret it for a very long time. Remember that before you speak."

She pulled a small pouch out of her trouser pocket and opened it, motioning for Ranita to hold out her hand. When she inverted the pouch, a small disk fell into Ranita's palm. As soon as Ranita's fingers closed over the disk, the woman slipped the pouch back into her pocket. Tendrils of shadow swirled about her arms and legs, but before her face became wrapped in shadow, she gave Gilad a piercing look.

"The music," she said. Her voice was soft, wistful. "Don't stop playing."

Before he could answer, she translated into shadow and slid away through the opening in the ceiling. The edges of the darkness she had become blurred and shimmered against the starlit sky.

"Did you see that?" Gilad asked, shuttering the beam of his torch. "That flash of light?"

"A star glimmered as she passed." Ranita let her voice betray her skepticism.

"No. That wasn't a star. She's spinning light and doesn't even realize it."

"It looked like a star to me. You're imagining what you want to see. She's still a Dark Spinner. We've put our lives, and the lives of three other humans, in the hands of a Dark Spinner. Perhaps the lives of everyone we love."

"She won't betray us."

"How can you be sure?"

Gilad shrugged. "I'm not. But it's what I believe." He paused. "You don't share my belief. I get that. So, what are you going to do with the information she provided?"

"I haven't decided. Even if she gave me codes that will open the doors to the holding area and the cells, what, or who, will I find waiting for me when I use them?"

They stood in silence until the night darkness was almost complete. The stars visible in the ceiling gap appeared brighter every moment. At last, Gilad unshuttered his torch, pointing it toward the door, and took a step in that direction.

"We can read the disk in my skimmer. Do you want a ride back to Hikeet?"

"Yes. Maybe. Let's look at the data first, and then I'll tell you."

The chip the Dark Spinner had given Ranita contained a dozen sets of codes with directions, including one for setting a timed hold on the detention area lift. The data was succinct, with no spare descriptions or analysis, no tips on avoiding discovery, and no identifiers to reveal who had downloaded the files. After entering the information into the skimmer's computer, Gilad slid the chip into the incinerator, not waiting for it to self-destruct.

Ranita studied the codes and instructions on the passenger seat screen, aware of Gilad watching her. When she had committed it all to memory, he made her recite it three times as he had done with the Dark Spinner. Satisfied, he switched off the screen and reached out to touch her arm, drawing her gaze toward him.

"What will you do?" he asked for a second time. His eyes reflected the glow from the control panels. "Do you want a ride back to Hikeet? Shall I alert the safe house to send a transport for the prisoners?"

Ranita gave herself one last moment of indecision before she answered. "Yes, and yes. I don't trust the Dark Spinner or her numbers, but I don't have any other options. My mission is to free the prisoners. We knew it would be risky."

She paused, letting her thoughts move from doubt to the specifics of her mission. "Unless something comes up to change my mind, I'll go in after midnight, after the watch has changed. That will give anyone waiting for me time to wonder if I'm coming. We know the DS guards aren't very well trained. Uncertainty could work in my favor."

Gilad nodded. "If there aren't too many of them. But if they're expecting a rescue attempt, they might have put on extra guards. They could overwhelm you by sheer numbers."

"Agreed. Be sure to call in a high alert, so everyone can prepare in case this goes wrong. We might need medical help, or Abraham might need to initiate damage control if I'm captured."

She considered revealing her suspicions about the janitor but decided against it. Gilad might advise her superiors to abort the mission. Better to avoid that and retain control. Control to make her own decision about whether to proceed. She would observe the janitor, see how he reacted if she didn't appear, and only talk to him if she couldn't make a determination about him any other way.

"Understood." Gilad powered up the skimmer, engaging the cloak, and it rose above the ground. He touched a button on the control panel and organ music filled the cabin. In counterpoint to its majestic tones, Ranita heard again the longing in the Dark Spinner's voice, and she wondered at it.

Was it genuine or feigned? This was not something she could ascertain on such brief acquaintance. It didn't matter, anyway. She would use the codes later tonight if no new information came to light to change her mind, and she would either rescue the prisoners or become one herself.

Gilad dropped her in the same spot where he had met her that morning. She chose a swift route to the sculpture garden, then loitered on its edges, watching. After only a short time, a figure appeared among the statues. Slipping behind a large stone woman in flowing robes, Ranita peered from under the woman's outstretched arm until the figure walked into a swath of light splashing out from the First Ministry Building.

The old janitor. He walked back and forth, peering behind some of the sculptures. Ranita held her breath when he came close to her stone woman, but he turned away as his signal unit chimed. He pulled it from a pocket and answered it, near enough for Ranita to hear his side of the conversation clearly.

"No, I'm here now, as you instructed, but she's not here." He paused to listen. "I've done everything I can. If she doesn't show up, I wouldn't know where to look for her any more than you would." Another pause. "What about Bella?" His tone was sharper, edged with anger. "No, that's not any of my business. She made sure I understood that a long time ago." One last pause. "Fifteen minutes. Ok."

He slipped the signal unit back into his pocket and continued pacing the garden, moving away from Ranita. She let her breath out slowly, without sound. She remained as still as one of the statues, watching the janitor pace until, at last, he turned and strode from the garden.

He was planning something with someone. But what, and with whom?

Ranita followed him, keeping to the shadows, until she came to the edge of the garden. The janitor should have followed the paved path around to the side of the First Ministry Building, to the door reserved for human workers. Instead, he climbed the stairs to the stone porch that fronted the building. A Dark Spinner standing near the brightly lit entrance stopped him, then took his arm and guided him through the main front doors.

This entrance was used by top officials, who wielded authority from bright, windowed offices, and by anyone, mostly Dark Spinners, who had business with the Ministry. Could the janitor be going to plead for his granddaughter's freedom? At this time of the evening? Not likely. But what other business could he have there? And why would a Dark Spinner greet him almost as an equal?

9

— · —

ROB

R anita leaned against a pillar at the garden gate, her breath coming hard and fast. How could she attempt a rescue when all the information she had was suspect? Were the prisoners even truly prisoners?

She strode away from the First Ministry Building. Her feet carried her, by instinct more than intent, to the main dining district, and to the back alley behind the Red Peacock Café. Rob might know something that would help her sort everything out.

She arrived too early and paced for nearly an hour. She was tempted to slip through the café's back door and try to find Rob. But a conversation inside might not be secure, and it would be better if the café's staff didn't see her, so she resisted the urge and continued to wait.

When closing time finally came, she hid farther away than usual, in a recessed doorway two buildings up from the café. Again, as on the previous evening, Rob was the last to come out, and he looked around with an air of anticipation. He was expecting her. She stirred, ready to step out to meet him, then slunk back into her hiding spot.

Filled with sudden doubt, she shook her head to clear her thoughts. She trusted Rob. Didn't she? Was this unexpected hesitation just worry for his welfare?

She shrunk farther into the shadows, sinking to a squat and wrapping her arms around her knees, but it was too late for hiding. He heard her small movements and came and knelt in front of her.

"Hey, you," he said, his voice soft, questioning. "What are you up to?"

She shrugged, unsure how much to tell him. "Nothing. Just thinking. Trying to make some decisions."

"Did the janitor give you the information you need?"

"Some of it. My data is incomplete. I'm not sure I can proceed with what I have."

His mouth pulled into a frown. "What do you still need? Is there some way I can help?"

"I don't know. Probably not. It's more a matter of figuring out what to do with the information I have. To decide if I can trust it."

He made a small, startled movement, a jerk of the head that might mean nothing but made her wonder. Stifling the sudden urge to run, she let him take her hands when he reached for them, but she resisted when he tried to pull her closer. She wanted to see his face, as much as the dim light allowed, and judge his reactions.

He stroked her hands, as if to soothe her. Or placate her.

"What don't you trust?" he asked. "The janitor is a harmless old man who wants to help his granddaughter. I can't imagine what the problem could be."

Rob's voice matched his hands, soothing, hypnotic, pitched to calm her. Or lull her into complacency. Her mind screamed a warning, and she jerked her hands away. Standing, she linked her arm through his in the old way. In this familiar attitude, she felt more able to judge the tenor of his words, and the truth behind them.

They sauntered up the alley without speaking, but when they reached the street, Rob pulled her to a stop.

"What don't you trust?" His voice was more insistent this time.

Ranita hesitated. She wanted to ask Rob what he knew about the janitor, but the instinct that had been warning caution all evening was growing stronger. If Rob's connections to the old man were closer than he had let on, anything she said now might be relayed, first to the janitor and then to the Dark Spinners, as soon as she and Rob parted company.

And yet, she had to say something. Explain herself somehow, since she had been foolish enough to seek Rob out. She gave herself a mental kick for breaking the rules and getting emotionally involved with an informant. There was no time to come up with a backup story. Only one other thing came to mind.

Ranita hesitated, but Rob was watching her, waiting. "A Dark Spinner offered to help with something. A small thing," she added hastily. "In exchange for another small favor. Harmless from my end."

She knew as soon as the words left her mouth, they were a mistake. She was surprised to find the urge to protect the Dark Spinner was as strong as the need to keep the details of her mission secret.

Rob grabbed her arm, swinging around to face her. "A Dark Spinner! What foolishness is this?"

"What do you mean?"

"A Dark Spinner? How can you ask what I mean?" His hand tightened on her arm, making her wince. His gaze moved from her face to her arm, and he released her, dropping his hand to his side.

"It's only a small thing," she said. "Not that important." She grimaced at the lie. "I might not even use it. I'm trying to decide."

He took a step back from her. "Listen to yourself. Dark Spinners are scum. They can't be trusted. Ever. We've agreed on this for as long as I've known you. Or so I thought. But now I'm wondering if I know you at all."

"You do. I'm the same I've always been. But sometimes we have to do things in my line of work—things that are risky. We have to use people we wouldn't ordinarily trust." The words sat uneasily on her tongue, accusing her with their truth. She did use people. Rob. She had been using him for years. And the Dark Spinner woman. The woman's face intruded—hard, cynical, but then, unexpectedly, wistful. Ranita hoped Gilad had given her accurate coordinates for Luxera. Hoped she would find the way to the light she longed for.

Rob took another step back but leaned forward a little to peer into her face. "Don't do it, Ranita. It won't turn out well. Either for you or for us."

Ranita's heart pounded, and she could hear the blood rushing past her ears. She trembled. She wanted to reach out to Rob, to grab him, to hold him, to promise to be wise and reasonable and always listen to him. But the expression on his face stopped her. His eyes were narrowed and glinted coldly in the dim light of a nearby streetlamp. His lips twisted into a sneer. There was no warmth there. No doubt. Only unyielding certainty and revulsion.

Had her face looked like that in the past whenever she spoke of Dark Spinners? She had felt the revulsion. No denying that. An image flashed into her mind—a Dark Spinner with red hair and orange eyes lying in a pool of blood. Had his eye flecks been silver? That part was a little fuzzy. The shadows that swirled around him dissipated as the life ebbed out of him. She could see her own hand, held out in front of her, grasping a laser pistol.

But she couldn't see her own expression. She had never thought about how she might appear when confronted with the darkness of the DS. Probably much like Rob now.

Ranita didn't want to see this reflection of her own ugliness. She would much rather look like Gilad with his open expression and kind gaze. He saw past his preconceptions, something Ranita had never been able to do. She averted her eyes from Rob's face, looking at the building looming behind him, mostly dark at this late hour, with a stray window lit up here and there.

"Hmph." Rob's voice held disgust and impatience. "I see where you're going with this. I thought you had better judgment." He reached out and gripped her shoulder. "Think hard about what you do. It may seem like a small thing, but once you start down this path, there'll be no going back. If you come to your senses, you know where to find me. If not . . ."

She understood. His form passed her in a blur as he headed for the next street, where he would catch his transport to Skakeet City. Tears threatened to spill from full eyes; she wiped them away with a brusque swipe of one hand. There was no time for emotional turmoil tonight. With a dangerous job to do, she needed to keep her focus. She hunched her shoulders inside her jacket, stuck her hands in its pockets, and trudged back through the dining district, trying to act nonchalant as she regathered her thoughts.

Even if fraternizing with informants wasn't off-limits, coming to see Rob had been a mistake. Unable to trust him enough to ask the questions that needed answers, she had instead told him the one thing that was sure to turn him against her. He hadn't asked her for details of her exchange with the DS, something he should have done if he planned to join the janitor in betrayal. That alone was almost enough to convince her he was trustworthy. But he was no longer hers.

10

—·—

INFILTRATION

The lonely realization that she had lost Rob's affection marched with Ranita through dark, deserted streets. They had seemed well matched: of similar ages, both unattached, and of like mind. His hatred of Dark Spinners had resonated with her. She had agreed with him wholeheartedly. Why had that changed now?

It was more than a need for the detention area access codes. If Ranita had not gotten involved with the DS woman, another plan might have come to her. She was resourceful and always found a way to complete her missions.

No. It was something about the woman herself. Despite Ranita's distrust, entrenched from long experience, there was something deep inside that wanted the DS to be, in reality, as she presented herself. A hope, however dim, that a Dark Spinner might want to seek the light.

Ranita shook off that idea. It warranted further examination, but not now. Now she would use the Dark Spinner woman's codes, but she would keep her mind open and prepared for any difficulty. If the DS woman had set a trap for her, she must not be caught in it.

By the time Ranita neared the First Ministry Building, she had regained her equilibrium. The clock in a tower down the street struck midnight. If the janitor's information was accurate, a change of guards would be taking place, followed by a round of security checks. On a normal night, those would take just short of twenty minutes. Then the guards would settle into their stations. It would be the opportune time for infiltration.

But Ranita could not count on this being a normal night. She waited well past the twenty minutes, working through her plans in the interim. The janitor's disk had contained a map of one route through the building to the detention area lifts. If he had been trustworthy, Ranita could have counted on that being the best route—the fastest and the safest.

It would be neither if he was in collusion with the Dark Spinners.

Ranita smiled grimly. There was more than one way through the old building. The janitor could not know of the times she had walked those halls on past missions and the information she had gleaned from other agents.

She checked her digital time piece. Just a little longer, now. She advanced to the side of the building. She could see the outline of the small door that would respond to her codes. It was dark, silent, unattended, at least on this side.

She fidgeted, anxious to get moving. One last review of the codes, and she moved to the door. Her hand shook as she lifted it toward the dimly lit panel above the door handle. She shook her head, pausing to steady herself. She was losing her edge. It really was time to retire.

Pushing the thought aside, Ranita let her fingers caress the smooth, cool buttons on the panel, then punched in the first code. She braced for the sound of alarms, prepared to run. But the panel made only a quiet beep and the handle clicked. Ranita grabbed it, pulled the door open, and slipped inside.

The short entrance corridor was deserted. Ranita expelled the breath she had been holding and tried to quiet the wild beating of her heart. She needed to get a grip on her emotions, or this mission would be a disaster even if all her information was correct and secure. She murmured a short supplication to Ya-Lohim, asking for calm and focus. With another deep breath, she stepped into the halls of the First Ministry Building with a firm, silent tread, alert for any movement, but no longer afraid.

Faint sounds drifted to her from behind and ahead. A door clicked shut somewhere. Feet whispered across the floors. A loud exclamation was cut off by a quick, quiet command. The sounds seemed to move, changing directions as Ranita crossed one intersecting hall, turned down another, passed yet a third.

She had doubtless been spotted on security cameras as soon as she entered. She must neutralize those before delving deeper into the building. The janitor had not provided information about power boxes and switches, but she knew where some of them were from the reports of other agents. The nearest was secreted in a supply closet a little beyond the next intersecting corridor.

She found the closet without difficulty. It was a narrow space, and stuffy, but she squeezed in and pulled the door closed. Her tiny artificial torch, one of the few tools she carried, provided sufficient light to illuminate the closet shelves. They were crammed with cleaning and sanitary supplies.

She knew the approximate placement of the panel and could guess which shelf to empty, but she struggled to remove the items and find another place for them in a space so tight she could barely bend or turn. Trying to lower a large bottle of liquid cleaner to the floor, she lost her grip and dropped it with a loud thump.

She waited, immobile, scarcely even breathing, for a long time after that, listening for sounds of discovery, expecting the door to jerk open at the hands of Dark Spinner guards at any moment. When the pounding of her heart finally eased and she was still alone in the dark closet, she began removing the rest of the items. The glow of the panel lights soon confirmed she had chosen the correct shelf.

A row of buttons took care of the cameras for the corridors in this wing of the building and a portion of the building's core. That should be sufficient. There was a similar panel in another closet on the far side of the building. Several agents had used it when infiltrating through the employee entrance. But Ranita didn't intend to go to that section of the building if she could help it. She could not get out that way, since the doors there required codes she did not have.

Now for the lights. They required a code, which her Dark Spinner informant had provided, and a series of instructions. Turn off all lights in eastern wing? Yes. Duration of outage? Three hours? That should give her enough time.

But the panel would not accept three hours. Ranita tried two hours, but again her instruction was denied. Finally, when she tried one hour, the panel beeped at her, and the indication light turned from green to red. An hour to traverse the corridors, find the prisoners, and get back out. It would be close, but it would have to do.

She searched for a menu that would control the lights in the detention area, but no matter what menu items she chose, there seemed to be no way to turn those lights off. And she was wasting seconds of her precious hour. There must be a control panel somewhere closer to that area. She would try to find it if and when she got that far.

Satisfied she had done all she could here, she switched off her torch and slipped out of the tiny closet. The corridor was dark now, but it took her eyes only a moment to adjust after the dim light of her torch and the control panel. A shout, hastily stilled, came to her from far away, but otherwise the corridors were quiet. The guards were regrouping, equipping themselves with hand-held lights and extrapolating her possible location based on the last glimpse they had of her before the cameras went dark. She must be far from this area by the time they arrived, looking for her.

Though the overhead lights were out, door control panels and indicator lights on the air filtration vents still glowed, providing Ranita just enough light to find her way. She walked, from long practice, with muted footfalls. Unencumbered by weapons or other gear, she could drift like half-spun shadow, light and swift. When she came to an intersection, she paused to consider her path. A murmur of voices came to her from straight ahead, the direction she had intended to take. So, a right turn here, instead.

Most of the voices fell away, but a trio of separate tones came to her more clearly from up ahead. Backtracking was not an option; that way led to the busier parts of the building. Hugging the wall, Ranita took advantage of its deeper shadow until she came to the next intersection. The voices grew louder, coming from the corridor to the right. Light came from that direction also, waving, flickering. Most likely, a guard wore a wrist torch. One voice hushed the others with a sharp command as Ranita flitted across the open space.

Surging into the deeper dark of the unlit corridor beyond the intersection, she felt for the wall, fearful she would crash into it and betray her location. When her fingers grazed the wall's smooth surface, she turned and flattened her back against it and remained motionless, trying to control her breathing. The silence stretched out. Ranita shivered with tension, and her leg twitched. Forcing herself to hold it still, she turned her head a little, angling her ear toward the hall. A scuffling noise warned of movement from that direction.

"Did you hear something?" a voice asked in a harsh whisper.

"I thought I saw someone. There in the middle of the hall," another voice said.

"Lasers set to kill," a third voice commanded.

"Kill!" It was the first voice, louder this time. "Sir, are you sure?"

Even with its quiet tones, the contempt in the leader's voice was evident. "Yes, kill. As per my briefing, they're just humans. Death is all such vermin are fit for."

"Are those our orders from above, sir?" The first voice was quieter this time, but its tone was firm.

"Those are *my* orders."

"What were our orders from Commander Vallier?"

Now the second voice spoke again. "I think they want prisoners to question. We should use stun setting."

"Quiet, both of you, and do as you're told. You two have probably already warned our quarry away, but let's go find out."

"Not until I know our orders, sir," the first voice said. "I'm not going to kill anyone on your word alone."

"You're questioning me? Do you want to face the committee and explain your insubordination?"

There was a moment of silence, then the dissenting voice spoke in clear tones, shedding the hushed near-whisper of the previous comments. "Better that than to kill on the basis of your hatred alone. Better a life in prison, or a death sentence, than to take a life just because the victim is human."

Ranita stifled a gasp. Could she be hearing this? How thoroughly her assumptions about Dark Spinners were being shattered, and all within the space of a single day. First by a woman who took significant risks because she wanted to spin light rather than shadow. And now by this guard, who was putting his life on the line to avoid wanton killing.

The sound of movement from the other hall shook Ranita free of her musings. The three guards would come her way at any moment, with laser pistols, or perhaps with more powerful weapons. At least one of them would have his weapon set to kill. And she was unarmed, with nowhere to hide.

Keeping her ear angled to catch any further conversation or sound of movement from her foes, Ranita slid her feet sideways across the floor, keeping her back pressed against the wall and trying to blend in. At about six paces, a door recess offered a hiding place. Better yet, the door handle gave way at a soft tug and the door cracked open.

A loud thump echoed from the other corridor. As Ranita pushed the door wider, the whine of a laser pistol echoed through the halls. She ducked, expecting to see a burst of light close by, or even feel its searing beam pierce her body. But the dim flash of light that caught her eye came from the other hall, followed by a moan.

"That's what we do to traitors who defend humans." The leader did not try to hush his voice or disguise his disgust. "Come on, now. Let's go do our job. Kill setting."

11

—·—

SHADOWED CORRIDORS

R anita slid through the door and eased it closed, careful not to let the handle click. The top half of the door contained a glass pane. She crouched below it and looked around, hoping for a better place to hide. The room was dark; if she moved too far, she might knock into furnishings and make a racket. Her best hope was to move to the side of the door, beyond the sight lines through the glass pane, and prepare to spring at anyone coming through. The guards would have to enter one at a time. She might have a chance.

The beam from an artificial torch flashed into the room through the door's glass. Voices sounded in the hall outside, the words muffled. Ranita stood, every muscle coiled and ready, and watched the light flash back and forth, aimed first down the dark hall, and then back toward the intersection. The guards spoke more loudly, bringing her isolated words and phrases. "Gone," one said, and then, "Too long . . . as expected . . . had to deal with traitor."

The voice faded and the light beams dimmed as the guards moved farther along the hall. Surely, they had noticed the door. They must have assumed their quarry had moved on. How careless of them. Ranita allowed herself a half-grin. Anyone so eager to kill was prone to mistakes.

When the corridor had been dark and quiet for several minutes, she grasped the doorknob and turned it with deliberate care. She didn't want to be the one making the mistakes tonight. Outside the door, she kept her back to the wall and side-stepped again, heading back toward the corridor intersection. The light here was brighter than it should have been, now that the guards had gone. As she eased around the corner into the intersecting corridor, Ranita saw the reason. An artificial torch lay on the floor, abandoned.

A low moan caused Ranita to revise her assessment. The owner of the torch was still here, sprawled on the floor. She approached warily, her nostrils flaring at the lingering stench of burned flesh overlaid with a coppery tang.

The Dark Spinner, lying in a pool of his own blood, was young. Too young to die. But die he must, and soon. A laser blast had torn away much of his right side. Cauterization had not held; the super-heated liquid in his body had burst the dam, and he was bleeding out fast.

He was pale, even in this dim light, and his eyes, staring up at her, were beginning to dull. The silver eye flecks caught the light, their pattern of movement too slow to follow. A wisp of shadow swirling around his torso faded as Ranita watched.

An eerie silence had fallen over the corridors. Armed men and women roamed through them, but the absence of telltale sound made it hard to focus on them or remember their significance. The mission, the danger, her animosity toward Dark Spinners, all fell away. This young man, dying because he had objected to killing without cause, was all that mattered.

Ranita knelt beside him. After a moment's hesitation, she took his hand. She couldn't recall ever having touched a Dark Spinner before, except in a fight. This hand was cool and clammy. She wanted to drop it and cringe away. But having begun to give comfort, it would be wrong to pull away, so she hung on.

The hand responded to her touch with a slight pressure, then went limp. Was he gone? No. His eyes were open, his gaze fastened on her face.

"Leave light," he murmured. "Want . . ."

"Yes." Ranita gave his hand a slight squeeze.

"Don't know . . . why. Light . . . not . . . for me." He grimaced and his eyes fluttered shut, but then popped back open. They searched Ranita's face, as if looking for confirmation of his statement.

"You're wrong," she said. "The light is for everyone. Ya-Lohim will take anyone into the light that desires it."

"Hope so."

His eyes still sought hers. Her face was too tense to force a smile, so she squeezed his hand again instead. He did not return the pressure. His eyes fluttered closed. His breathing was rapid and shallow.

Ranita studied him. Her mind whirled with half-formed thoughts, conflicting emotions. Dark Spinners were the scum of the world, dammed by their rejection of Ya-Lohim. And yet, she had just welcomed this one into the light. How could this be?

Sound, echoing from distant corridors, filtered back into her awareness and, with it, a renewed sense of urgency. This man's comrades knew someone was here, or at least suspected it. Guards would be looking for her. The Dark Spinner still lived, but death would claim him soon and he would not rouse to consciousness again before the end. She could offer him no further help or comfort. And she needed to free the prisoners before the next change of the watch.

She left his torch lit as she hurried away from him. The path she had originally chosen was now open to her, but it was difficult to discipline her thoughts for the task ahead. The eyes of the dying Dark Spinner kept disrupting her sight lines, and the sound of his failing breath whispered to her around every corner.

It was instinct, rather than clear thinking, that guided her to the room the janitor had marked as high security, from which she could access the detention levels. To get there, she dodged several patrols of guards. The building was much busier than it should have been at this time of night. Which meant they were expecting an infiltration. Guards would be posted near the detention lift. A fight was coming.

It was this expectation, and the ensuing surge of adrenaline, that helped Ranita finally banish thoughts of the young man she had left dying in the hallway. Her mind snapped into focus as she rounded the last corner, prepared to rush the enemy.

But no one was there. The only barrier ahead was a large metal door, solid and imposing. She raised her hand to the code panel, then paused, wondering again about the Dark Spinner woman's motivations. Giving access to the building was one thing, giving access to the detention area quite another. Surely, a trap waited behind this door.

But coming this far was pointless if she didn't continue. Ranita entered the number-letter combination and waited, holding on to her calm by sheer determination. A faint buzz emanated from the door, and it responded to her tug, opening easily.

Inside, a small, well-lit room contained only a counter along the left side, with an unoccupied stool behind it. A door behind the counter had a glass pane inserted in its top half. The brightness of the outer room nearly absorbed the dim glow spilling through the pane. Another door, across from the main entrance, was smooth save for a split down the middle, and had no handle. A lift, most likely to the detention levels. With another keypad beside it.

Ranita spotted a panel on the wall behind the counter to the left of the door. The control panel for the lights in this section? She took one step toward it, then stopped and looked around for cameras. She found four, all mounted high in the corners of the room, but their indicator lights were dull. Her earlier manipulations of the surveillance system had apparently deactivated these cameras along with those in the corridors.

Which meant no one knew she was here. If she turned out the lights and someone, either a clerk or guard, came into the room while she was down at the cells, they might suspect she had been here and would be waiting for her when she returned. Better to leave the lights on and leave her adversaries guessing.

A burst of feminine laughter emanated from behind the glass-paned door. Ranita could make a good guess where the clerk was who should have been sitting at the counter. Another mistake. It might have been better if the clerk was sitting at the counter where Ranita could incapacitate her at once. Better than having to deal with her on the way back through with the freed prisoners.

On the other hand, if she passed through without a confrontation now, leaving no damaged furniture or unconscious bodies, there would be no clues to her presence in the detention section. And if her adversaries could make a mistake of this magnitude here, in this sensitive area, might not more mistakes be forthcoming? The lack of training and discipline among the Dark Spinner guards was turning into an asset.

Ranita crouched below the level of the counter as she passed the door, not rising back to her full height until she reached the lift. She punched in the next code and waited again, this time with a sense of expectation. For the first time, she dared to believe the Dark Spinner had kept her side of the bargain—had given accurate information. That didn't mean she hadn't set a trap somewhere ahead, but it did not surprise Ranita when the doors slid wide to reveal a well-lit, empty compartment.

She stepped in and recoiled. Someone was here, hidden against the side wall. She jumped back, and the other person jumped as well. Ranita uttered a low exclamation that bordered on hysterical laughter, then clamped a hand over her mouth, remembering the clerk in the adjacent room. She stepped back into the lift, and the other person stepped back with her. She faced herself; turning, she saw her image reflected again on the other side wall.

12

— · —

INTERROGATION FIVE

J ust mirrors. They revealed a disheveled, wild-eyed woman with heightened color, looking nothing like a calm, experienced agent. Ignoring her reflection, Ranita touched the button for Interrogation Five.

As she rode down, she reviewed the janitor's information about this lowest, most secure area. A short corridor with an interrogation room on each side. An intersecting corridor with four holding cells. That was all, unless the old man had deliberately left out vital information.

The lift had made only half its descent. To keep her mind distracted for the rest of the trip down, Ranita examined the mirrors. They were not flush with the walls, but were mounted so that they stood out about two centimeters. She ran her finger along the edge of one. She could just get a grip. It might be possible to jerk on it hard enough

102

to break a piece off if she needed a weapon. A mirror shard didn't seem like much of a weapon against a Dark Spinner, but sometimes the smallest things made the difference.

The lift came to rest on the lowest level, and the silent doors slid open. She entered the short code to hold the lift in place with the doors open. Then she leaned forward to peer out. The doors to the interrogation rooms, one on each side of a short hall, rose like menacing sentinels. Light fixtures at the tops of the doors were dark. Good. No interrogations in progress right now. She just needed to find her prisoners and get out before someone came to check on them.

Ranita could see two of the cell doors on the far wall of the intersecting corridor. The other two doors would be further along the hall, one at each end. She had codes to all four doors, but she hoped she wouldn't have to open all of them. The lift doors would hold open for five minutes. She had that long to open the correct holding cells and convince the prisoners to follow her. If the lift closed, there would be another five-minute delay before she could open them again.

She raced to the one of the visible doors. It was solid metal, but there was a little window at eye level covered by a metal plate that slid open at the touch of a lever. Glass created a barrier to sound, but not to sight. A quick scan of the cell assured Ranita that its two cots were empty. She clicked the lever to close the window and hurried to the next cell at that end of the hall.

Also, empty. Would they keep all the prisoners in one cell? Or maybe the two men were together. Turning to the other end of the hall, she checked the third door. Only one cot in here and it was empty. At one or two cots per cell, she was unlikely to find all three prisoners. Had she done this for nothing?

The lift beeped a warning. One minute gone. One more door. As soon as the metal plate slid away from the last window, she saw faces she recognized. A man with graying hair and a lined face slept on a cot. Jacob. He had been tough to recruit, cautious by nature and hesitant to make a commitment. He had finally come to the safe house just a week ago, and already his worst fears had been realized. Despite this, he appeared peaceful. She could see no obvious sign of injury. No bruises that might indicate he'd been tortured. Was it possible the interrogator hadn't started on him yet?

The younger man, Willem, almost a stranger to her, sat on another cot with head bowed. His mouth moved, as if he was talking to himself. Or praying. He, too, appeared unharmed, though his hands rubbed his legs and his left foot jiggled, the constant motion betraying his lack of calm.

An unexpected third cot in the room was unoccupied. Bella was missing.

Ranita's heart skipped a beat, and her mind swirled. If all three had been here, the rescue would have proceeded as planned. If none of them had been here, she would have started over, gathering information. But now? Rescuing the men would put Bella in greater peril, and any information she had about the resistance community would be at risk. And making a second attempt for Bella after taking the men out would be extremely hazardous.

The lift beeped again. The second minute gone. Three more in which to make a decision and act on it. She tapped on the glass, and Willem lifted his head and stared at the door, then stood. His mouth moved, but Ranita couldn't hear what he said. She wouldn't be able to communicate through the glass. Willem's mouth moved again, and Jacob stirred on his cot.

Ranita's fingers reached for the keypad, then hesitated. She had four codes, one for each door, but which was which? Was this door the first or the last on the list? Farthest to the left, as a guard would enter. Did that make it the first door? And would a wrong code set off an alarm? She fumbled with numbers, almost forgot a letter, as she punched them in.

The lock clicked. She grabbed the handle and pulled before it could decide there was an error and lock her out. The door swung out. Both men stared at her with bewildered expressions. The lift beeped again. Two minutes left.

"Where's Bella? I'm supposed to bring all three of you out."

Jacob recovered from his surprise first. "They took her to interrogation a while ago. Should be back by now, I'd think." His eyes reflected his worry.

"Interrogation at this time of night?" A picture of the dark lights above the interrogation rooms flashed through Ranita's mind. Had she missed something?

"Is it night?" Jacob asked in a strangely uncurious voice. "Doesn't matter much, night or day, down here. Taking you at unexpected times, that's part of how they break you."

"Do you know how long she's been gone?"

"Hard to tell."

Willem leaned forward, eager with his answer. "I've been keeping track. About two hours."

"How do you know that?" Jacob asked.

"Easy. I've sung through the Lightbringer's Anthem more than twenty times. Takes five minutes, unless I've sung too fast or slow."

Shock coursed through Ranita, and her heart pounded. "Lightbringer's . . . How do you know that? No one teaches it anymore."

"Someone's teaching it. Heard it, out Clearwater way. Some children were outside singing. I liked the sound, so I snuck close to listen. It was some sort of class or practice, and they sang it several times. Enough for me to remember, except a few words I can't get right."

Ranita stared at him. Clearwater was a farming village, part of her secret community. Willem, stumbling across it, had come too close to the hidden parts of the community. If he revealed what he had heard to an inquisitor, it would give the Dark Spinners a clue. They might not know the anthem, but they would understand what it meant, who would sing it. It might be the first step in the road to discovery.

The lift beeped again. One minute left. Time to decide.

"Come with me. We have to go now if I'm going to get you out of here tonight."

Willem started forward, but Jacob hesitated. "What about Bella?" he asked.

"I don't know. I'll figure it out later. Come on, now. I can't let the inquisitors get to you."

She started back toward the lift, turning once to motion them after her. Willem followed her closely. Jacob came more slowly behind them.

As she and Willem entered the lift, it uttered a series of warning beeps. Ranita leaned out and seized Jacob's arm, pulling him into the lift as the doors started to close. He stared at her, wide-eyed, while she entered the code for the main level. As they rode up, Ranita felt tension spread through her shoulders and into the rest of her body. Her presence in the security area would have been hard to explain before. Now, with two prisoners in tow, it would be impossible. If the clerk had returned to the counter, she must be ready to make her explanation by force.

As the lift slowed, she caught herself holding her breath. She expelled it slowly, and took another breath, slow and deep, fighting for calm. She glanced once at the mirror to her right, then focused on coiling her muscles, ready for anything, or nothing.

The doors slid open, revealing a couple clinging to one another in a passionate embrace. The man lifted his mouth away from the woman's enough to murmur, "The lift, finally. Thought it'd never . . ." He cut off abruptly as he angled his head enough to see the three in the lift. He pushed the woman away from him and straightened. Tendrils of shadow wreathed his hands and coiled around his feet and legs. His eyes narrowed. "Who are you? What are you doing with those prisoners?"

"Bella!" Jacob's voice cut through the man's questions. "What are you doing? With the inquisitor? Traitor!"

13

FLIGHT

Ranita took one startled look at the woman's face, recognizing the finely molded features and the silky raven hair, also recognizing the guilt and defiance there. Then the inquisitor himself, and no mere clerk, moved, blocking her view of the girl. The shadows swirled up from his legs to his torso. The handle of a weapon formed in his right hand.

"Didn't believe the old man," he muttered. "Thought no one would be this foolish."

"Surprise," Ranita said as he stepped into the lift, reaching for her. His weapon, a shadow-wrapped sword, elongated and tilted toward her. She eluded the lengthening blade, springing to her right and turning to get a good angle for her fingers on the mirror. With a desperate jerk, she broke off a large piece. Glass shattered, spraying the lift floor.

She ignored it as light caught her attention. The mirror fragment, waving wildly in her hand as she side-stepped away from the inquisitor's second lunge, reflected light from the lift's ceiling panel and from the brightly illuminated room beyond. Its flash glittered on the walls of the lift, doubled in the opposite mirror, caught in the inquisitor's eyes. With a harsh exclamation, he threw up an arm as a shield. He wore no jacket, only a tunic of thin fabric with mid-length sleeves that left his lower arm exposed. Ranita slashed at the bare arm with her mirror shard, tearing into the flesh, ripping it open.

The inquisitor gasped. His weapon disintegrated as his other hand came up to grasp the jagged wound. Blood flowed from it, spattering Ranita, the men with her, the lift. The tendrils of shadow dissipated. The inquisitor hugged the wounded arm against his chest. Giving him no chance to recover, Ranita kicked the inside of his knees, and he collapsed to the floor with a grunt.

She pushed Jacob out of the lift. "Get Bella. Hold on to her. Keep her quiet. Willem, open the door." She grabbed Willem's arm and pushed him after Jacob, even as she stomped her foot in the middle of the inquisitor's back. "I don't know how long I can keep him down. Hurry."

Bella screamed as Jacob grabbed her, nearly covering the sound of Willem's voice.

"The door's locked," Willem shouted. "I can't open it."

"The code." Ranita shook her head, trying to concentrate. The inquisitor was moving, trying to get up. He got his knees under him. Then his good arm. He paused, swaying on three limbs, and gave his head a shake, as if trying to clear his mind. He uttered the deep snarl of a wild animal. A cornered, angry animal.

Ranita dropped her mirror fragment and made a double fist. The inquisitor lifted his blood-spattered face to look at her, the snarl twisting his lips, just as she brought her hands down. Her blow caught his left temple, and he collapsed. The snarl changed to a groan, and he lay still.

The code. Willem was watching her, expectant. She reached into her memory, grateful for the many times she had reviewed the codes. "Enter this. 1, 3, 3, L, 2, 3, 3, S, 3, 7. Got that?"

She didn't have to wait for an answer. Willem pushed buttons as she spoke, and a moment after she finished, in the pregnant pause of anticipation, she heard the door buzz. Willem grabbed the handle and shoved it open.

"Go," Ranita shouted. She gave the inquisitor a parting kick, aiming for his kidneys. Even unconscious, his body flinched away from the blow. As he turned, she got a good look at his arm. It was bleeding hard enough that he would bleed out if no one found him soon.

She shuddered. She had killed before, one time. And had vowed never to kill again. It might be better if this man didn't survive to identify her. But if she had killed him? Another shudder shook her whole body, but Jacob and Willem were watching her from outside the door, waiting for directions. Jacob held one hand over Bella's mouth while his other arm circled her waist, trying to control her squirming. There was no time for Ranita to indulge her qualms.

She punched in the code to hold the lift doors open. Then she grabbed the stool from behind the counter and wedged it into the open door to the outer hallway to hold that door open. If someone arrived in the next five minutes, they would find him and he might survive. It was all she could do for him.

The corridor outside the detention area was still dark. Her hour was not yet up, though it felt like she had been roaming these hallways for an eternity. The lights would likely come back on soon. They needed to get as close to their exit as possible before that happened. Though it might not matter. If Bella didn't stop wailing, every guard in the place would know right where to find them.

As soon as they got beyond sight of the detention area, Ranita paused long enough to tear a strip of cloth from the bottom of her tunic. Willem took it and gagged Bella with it, securing it with a tight knot at the back of her head. She struggled so hard, Jacob was forced to push her against the wall, face forward, to keep her still enough for Willem to tie his knot.

Ranita's stomach twisted, watching them. How was she going to get out of the building with a prisoner fighting all the way, making enough noise to alert every guard in the place? But the two men were efficient. With grim expressions and no attempt at gentleness, they each took one of Bella's arms and pulled her along.

Ranita led them back along the same route she had used on her way in. When she saw the light from the fallen Dark Spinner's torch, she quickened the pace and tried not to look at him. But the footsteps behind her faltered, and as she turned to motion the others on, she glimpsed the man's face. He was dead now, but not with the ghastly stare and pain-twisted features she had feared. His eyes were closed, his expression serene. She slowed, letting her gaze linger on his face for an instant before hurrying the others forward. They edged around him with wild eyes. Bella struggled harder and moaned against her gag.

The outer door was near now. As Ranita strode through the halls, she reached up under her tunic and activated the signal beacon still secure around her waist, calling Gilad and the extraction team to move in. The codes for the outer door rumbled in Ranita's head, and her fingers itched with readiness to punch them into the keypad.

The rumble of marching feet, echoing from the right-hand corridor, brought her to an abrupt halt. She braced her feet as her companions hurtled into her, pushing hard against them to keep from stumbling into the next intersection. The murmur of feet stopped, and a voice issued crisp commands.

"Split up at the next intersection. You four, secure the side access door. Commander Vallier thinks the intruders came in that way. Might try to egress there. The rest, follow me. There's word of a man down in the back corridors. We need to check it out. Laser pistols ready, everyone."

Ranita spun and pushed the other three back the way they had come. Her escape route was cut off. Four armed guards held the door, while an additional force of unknown size was coming her way. With laser pistols. Maybe she should reconsider her refusal to carry a weapon.

But the thought brought a flash of memory—that red-headed Dark Spinner in a pool of blood, dropped by her own laser gun. Never again. Taking care of one's enemy by laser was too easy.

On the other hand, getting out of a building crawling with armed guards would not be easy—it would be next to impossible. And she didn't have the access codes for the employee entrance on the far side of the building. That meant there was only one route left to her.

It was crazy. She knew that. That Dark Spinner woman must have known it, too. Had she given up the codes knowing she wasn't really betraying her own kind? Knowing that there would be too many guards and Ranita would never make it out. And that last code? The most impossible one of all.

Ranita made a quick right turn into a corridor that was, for the moment, deserted. It led back into the inner recesses of the building. A veritable dead-end. But she knew, as the Dark Spinner would have known, that she could not use that last code. The door it opened would be guarded both inside and out. She and the others would be dead or imprisoned as soon as they tried it. The Dark Spinner had known Ranita would be caught, no special trap needed.

Or had she?

Ranita skidded to a stop, and the others crashed into her once again. She braced her hand against the wall to keep from being knocked over. Jacob and Willem stared at her, their eyes narrowed in confusion. Bella started squirming again and making noises through her gag. Ranita tried to ignore her as she gathered her thoughts.

Did she have any other options? None came to mind. She had never trusted her Dark Spinner informant. But that was only because she didn't trust any Dark Spinner. The woman's face, one moment cynical, the next wistful, flashed through her memory. Every code Ranita had tried so far had worked. There had been no traps. Was it time to trust? Had the DS woman earned that?

Help! She let the cry echo in her mind, trusting Ya-Lohim to hear. And then she reversed directions, charging past the others, pivoting to the right at the next intersection, followed by a left turn and another left. She chose her route according to the sounds of feet and voices that wafted to her through the halls, and through an instinctual sense of direction. Her destination was fixed in her mind, and after two more turns she found what she sought: the main corridor, leading straight to the entrance hall and the big front doors.

Ranita flew down the corridor, every nerve and muscle alert and ready for a fight, but the wide entrance hall was deserted. Where were the guards? Roaming the corridors, looking for her? She would no doubt have to fight her way through guards outside, but for now, she had a much-needed interlude with time to assess the situation and figure out how to use the code.

"Thank you," she whispered as she examined the room.

A few dimmed light panels on the side walls provided enough illumination for Ranita to see the wide double doors that led out to the stone porch at the front of the building. She stepped near to them and felt the others pressing close behind her. Bella had stopped struggling. Ranita glanced over her shoulder, checking to make sure the men had not relaxed their grip. Even in the dim light, she could read their grim expressions well enough to know she didn't need to worry. If they made it out, they would bring Bella with them. She turned her attention to the door, searching for a code panel, with its rows of numbers and letters, smooth and cool, waiting to welcome her fingers.

There wasn't one.

But there had to be. She had the code. She started to tremble, and her mind raced as adrenaline surged. Was this the trap her Dark Spinner informant had set?

No. She wouldn't believe that. Not after so many right codes. Not after coming so far. There must be a way to use the code, if she could think clearly long enough to find it. What was she missing?

Stepping closer, she ran her hand up and down the wall along the left side of the doors. Nothing.

Voices floated to her from other parts of the building. They were louder, closer. Was there something she could ram the doors with?

Ranita shook that thought away as useless and stepped to the right side of the doors. This time, when she ran her hand along the wall, her fingers found a raised area, round and lined with ridges. On one side, she detected a bump that might be a button. There was no way to punch a multi-digit code in with just one button, but the voices from the corridors were louder, getting close, so she pressed the button.

Light sprang up behind the circular area, illuminating it, and Ranita recognized a voice activation panel. A chill washed through her limbs, leaving her trembling. With silence her best defense, she was now required to speak the code? She leaned in until her mouth was only a few centimeters from the panel and recited the code in a shaky whisper.

"Code not detected," a woman's voice blared from the panel. "Please try again."

Ranita caught her breath and listened. Voices still rumbled somewhere in the far recesses of the building, but those that were close had stilled. The blaring voice from the panel would have alerted the closest pursuers to the presence of their quarry. They were listening now, trying to decipher precisely where the sound had come from. She balled her hand into a fist and aimed a blow at the doors but caught herself and pulled her arm back before the blow landed.

Venting frustration would not get her out of the building. She leaned toward the panel and repeated the code a little louder, then stepped back to wait for the doors to open.

"Incorrect," the woman's voice stated. "Please try again. Speak loudly and clearly."

Footsteps sounded a quick staccato along the main hallway, moving her way. The guards would be here in seconds, and then she and the three she had come to rescue would all be in detention. There would be no code panels on the insides of the cell doors. She grimaced. Correction. All but Bella would be in detention. Ranita surmised Bella's lover would give her better accommodations. If he survived.

Well, let them come. She wasn't done yet. Pulling herself up to her full height, she took a deep breath and spoke the code in crisp, ringing tones. As if her voice had the power of the Creator, bringing the sun, moon, and stars into glorious existence, a double bank of lights on the ceiling above suddenly blazed with light.

Her hour of darkness was up. She would be visible to any who followed her voice to the entrance hall. She couldn't stop them and there was no place to hide. She was in Ya-Lohim's hands.

She crossed her arms and waited, trying to ignore the seconds that ticked away, the pounding footsteps, the rough shout that told her the guards had sighted her and her companions.

14

— · —

A NOTABLE TRANSFORMATION

"Code accepted. Step away. Doors opening." The voice that had sounded hateful a moment before now seemed cheerful and friendly. With a welcome creak, the doors began to swing inward. But so slowly. And the rush of feet behind her warned Ranita that the Dark Spinner guards were just steps away from the entry room.

As soon as the opening between the doors was big enough, she stuck her hand between them and grabbed the right-hand door. It was heavy wood, nearly ten centimeters thick, unvarnished and rough to the touch. Ranita ignored the sharp prick of a splinter as she adjusted her grip and tugged with all her strength. The massive door didn't respond to her tug, but continued its slow, measured movement.

The opening was large enough to get her shoulder through now, and she leaned against the door, throwing her full weight into her efforts. Her push was ineffective at first, but then, suddenly, the door jerked. An instant later, it slammed against the side wall, accompanied by an agonized screech and a loud beeping from the voice activation panel.

Ranita stumbled at the door's sudden movement. She grabbed Willem's arm to steady herself. As soon as she regained her balance, she sprang through the wide opening, ignoring the beeping. Shouts greeted her on the porch outside, echoed by loud commands from inside the building.

"Halt! Surrender. Ready lasers."

Ranita lunged toward the nearest guard on the porch, shoving him to the ground before he could react to the onslaught. She turned in time to see another guard tumble as Jacob kicked her legs out from under her. Ranita ducked as a guard near the stairs fired a laser pistol at her. Jacob, Willem, and Bella were in front of her now, almost to the steps.

As Willem started the descent, dragging Bella with him, Jacob gave a cry and crumpled onto the stone porch floor. He grabbed his leg as he teetered on the edge of the stairway. Willem hesitated, and Bella nearly pulled out of his grasp.

"Go!" Ranita shouted at him. "I'll help Jacob. Run."

She grabbed Jacob's arm, urging him up, and flung her arm around his waist, supporting him as he struggled to his feet. She pulled him down the steps as a flash of laser fire passed over them. The next one might not miss. She moved faster, dragging Jacob with her, her feet moving so fast they barely touched the steps. Once, she stumbled and they both nearly fell, but the adrenaline that had been building in her through the halls of the First Ministry Building gave her strength. She found her footing just in time and ran on.

At the bottom of the stairs, two more guards confronted her. Only one held a laser. She swerved toward him, crashing into him before he could shoot. He dropped with a thud and a cry. The other guard sprang toward them. Ranita ran on, pulling Jacob with her, knowing she couldn't outrun the guard. Jacob tried to keep up, limping on a burned and bleeding leg, but he was slowing them down.

"Go without me." His voice was hoarse, and he gasped for breath. "I'll create a diversion for you."

"No. Don't stop. I came to get you. I won't leave you now."

The guard drew within an arm's length. Ranita tensed, preparing to drop Jacob and fight. A cry behind her caught in someone's throat and was cut off. Slowing, twisting, she glanced around to see the guard, just a step away, skid to a stop as tendrils of shadow crept up his body and engulfed him. Ranita stopped and stared, though she knew she needed to keep running. An arm flailed out of the shadow and she shuddered.

A spark of light caught her eye. And another. She stared harder. The shadow that spun around the guard changed slowly to spinning light.

It wasn't pure light. Shadows and random colors intermixed with the white of the light, forming erratic patterns. But it was still a wondrous sight. Ranita had never seen a Light Spinner. In her imagination they were a simple deviation of the Dark Spinners, an aberration, more attractive, but still wrong and repugnant. How misguided she had been, how backward her assessment. This spinning, even in its impure form, was right and true and uplifting.

Laughter bubbled up into her throat, but at Jacob's tug on her sleeve, she stifled it. He clung to her, near collapse, his trouser leg soaked with his blood. Firming her grip around his waist, she turned and ran again. Willem, with Bella in a tight grasp, waited for them near the entrance to the sculpture garden.

"In here." Ranita led the way into the garden. As she headed for the first sculpture, she turned again, just in time to glimpse a tendril of light undulating into the night sky. The shouts of guards behind her spurred her to keep moving; she wove through the statues, hoping their shadowy bulk would confuse her pursuers. Footfalls sounded louder behind her, and the raspy breath of running guards. One of them uttered a sharp cry. And then, inexplicably, as she neared the garden's far edge, the sounds of pursuit ceased.

She slowed, turning to look. Jacob slumped against her, his breathing shallow and labored. A shadow loomed up in front of her. Without hesitation, she let go of Jacob and sprang toward the shadowy figure, kicking out as she jumped. Just as quickly, her opponent reacted, leaping away from her rather than attacking.

She crouched, preparing to spring and kick again.

"Nita, stop! It's me, Gilad."

Ranita remained in her crouch, trying to make sense of the words, the urge to fight strong, blocking rational thought.

"Nita." The voice was softer. "It's all right. The extraction team has the others. Let them near so they can help your friend. We've got to get out of here."

Gilad's voice penetrated her defenses this time. She felt the sudden dump of adrenaline and trembled, swaying as she tried to straighten. Gilad jumped forward and caught her before she collapsed. She heard Jacob groan, felt movement as members of the extraction team lifted him and helped him away, toward the street. The light from a transport door spilled out momentarily, then disappeared. Only the hum gave away the location of the cloaked vehicle as it lifted into the air.

"Bella," Ranita said, regaining her focus at last. "The girl. Don't take her to the safe house with the others. Take her to Micah and his team. She's turned to the shadow. We need to find out how much she knows, what she told the inquisitor."

Gilad pulled a signaling device out of his pocket and spoke into it, issuing crisp commands. Then he put it away and linked his arm through Ranita's.

"Can you walk? My skimmer's on a back street nearby."

"Yes." Ranita drew in several deep breaths and felt her trembling subside to a manageable level. "Lead the way."

As they walked, Ranita became aware of shouts and flashing lights coming from the direction of the First Ministry Building. An alarm sounded in her mind, but it was unfocused, fuzzy. Gilad didn't appear concerned. Why should she be? They were safe in the dark, and his skimmer waited just ahead. As she collapsed into the passenger seat and Gilad brought the power online and engaged the cloak, he studied her with raised eyebrows.

"You've had quite a night," he said.

"Yes. They were expecting me, or someone like me, tonight. The place was crawling with DS guards."

"Oh? But it wasn't a problem with our Dark Spinner's codes?" He slid his hand across the control panel and the skimmer lifted away from the street.

"No," she said, her voice quiet. "Our Dark Spinner kept her bargain. She acted with more integrity than some of the humans involved. And I think . . ." She hesitated, trying to believe what she had seen. "I think she helped me there at the last, even though she was adamant that she wouldn't."

Gilad nodded. "I'm not surprised. I followed her to the university astronomy building. She must have decided the coordinates were worth more than just the codes. But tell me everything." He settled the skimmer into cruising speed and shifted to a more comfortable position in his seat.

Ranita told him the story in terse, clipped sentences.

"You think the janitor was in on things with his granddaughter, with Bella?" Gilad asked when she finished.

"I don't know. His data was accurate, but his behavior was suspicious. We should pick him up, if we can find him, and question him."

"I'll alert the team once everyone's well out of the extraction zone. How about you? Are you all right?"

"Yes. I think I'm going to have a harder time trusting anyone after this. Except . . ." She left the thought unfinished.

Gilad gave her a musing glance and nodded as he brought the skimmer down. Ranita looked around, taking in their surroundings. On one side of the skimmer, a wide-open countryside sparkled with stars. On the other side, a building loomed, dark but still majestic, its dome blocking out a space of starlight.

"The cathedral?" Ranita looked at Gilad in disbelief. "Is it really the time for this?"

He shrugged. "Just thought you might like a few moments to catch your breath and order your thoughts before we retrieve your skimmer and head home for debriefing."

"Yes. Thank you."

Ranita stepped out of the skimmer and drew in deep breaths of fresh air. She followed Gilad into the cathedral. He made his way to the organ in the dark and switched on the battery pack that powered the instrument. Its on-switch glowed green, the only light other than starlight. Gilad slipped onto the bench and fingered the keys, letting a slow, quiet melody waft out through the cathedral.

The music was soft enough Ranita didn't have to worry about it carrying beyond the nave. She sat below the dome and closed her eyes, the tranquil tones washing over her, cleansing the tension of the night from her muscles, drawing her toward sleep, toward peace.

Later, as she stood by the skimmer waiting for Gilad to let her in, she caught a flash of light near the cathedral dome, just above the opening in its roof.

"Did you see that?" she asked Gilad. "That light?"

"It was a star," he answered. "Nothing more."

"We both know it wasn't a star," she countered. "Someone who likes organ music is spinning light."

She smiled as she climbed into her seat, and felt the world shift in a transformation as great as that suffered by her state-of-the-art skimmer, now disintegrating at the bottom of the sea. This change was not a disintegration, however, but the integration of a new perspective.

Oh, there would be losses. Rob might be one if he could not ride the sea change with her. Her smile faltered. She only now realized how much she had counted on Rob being in her future. Being something more than an informant going forward. That was unlikely now. She missed him already.

And yet. And yet. She looked up at the sky, twinkling with starlight, and imagined a myriad of Light Spinners observing her world. She smiled with the rightness of that image. If one star seemed brighter than the others, moving as no star should, through the void, that was also well. Everything was as it should be, and nothing would ever be the same again.

THE END

ACKNOWLEDGMENTS

To my family and friends, and especially to my ever-supportive husband, thank you for your constant encouragement on this long journey to publication.

To my writing family, especially the Colorado Springs chapter of ACFW—thank you for being so positive and uplifting and always pointing the way along the writing path. Your advice has been invaluable. Even more important, having a group of friends I can meet with face to face, friends who understand the writing life, has kept me going over the years.

A special thanks to the ACFW COS chapter critique group—Diane Campbell, Alicia Whittle, and others. You've helped make this a better book.

Thank you to my editor, Annie Douglass Lima. Your edits boosted the book's quality and my confidence.

Thank you, Jenneth Dyke, for the fabulous cover design.

And finally, to my Creator and Lord, thank you for the gift of story, and for giving me grace, strength, and skill to tell the particular stories you have favored me with.

IF YOU ENJOYED THIS BOOK--

If you enjoyed *At the Boundary Between Daylight and Shadow*, please consider leaving a review at your favorite retail platform. It will help others find and enjoy this story. Thank you.

To get updates on new stories in the Seven World Dominion, sign up for Eileen's monthly newsletter at www.eileenrhickman.com. As a thankyou gift, you'll receive the free story, *Dragon Light,* which introduces you to the first world in the Dominion, Sek-Nar.

While you're at the website, check out the *Seven World Dominion* page to learn more about some of the worlds in the Dominion, including Ranita's world, Exalton. Or, to explore further, continue in this book for another Seven Worlds story.

FOR FURTHER READING

Turn the page to enjoy *Tendrils of Shadow*, another story from the Seven World Dominion, set on Luxera, the world of the Light Spinners.

Ayia stands poised on the cusp of a choice. Enticed by the shifting shadows that inhabit her mind and flow from her fingertips, she tries to resist, knowing Yellaz Prison awaits if she gives in to the temptation. And she is repelled by the casual abuse her brother, an avowed Dark Spinner, inflicts on his family. When he threatens to take his teen-aged children to a world where darkness reigns, Ayia is the only one who might stand in the way and provide a safe haven. But to save her niece and nephew from darkness, or even death, she needs to banish her own shadows. If she can.

— · —

TENDRILS OF SHADOW

A Story of the Seven World Dominion
From the Second World: Luxera
by Eileen R Hickman

Shadows tantalized Ayia from the corners of the room. She had been ready to reach for them for days. Only the concern that once she started, she might not be able to turn back had kept her from wrapping herself in them. Today the pull was stronger, but the presence of the children held her back.

No, not children anymore. They had grown up when she wasn't looking. Zeezia must be almost sixteen, and Keyar . . . ?

She stilled the motion of her rocking chair to study him. He stood across the room, near the door, his eyes focused on shapes his hands formed with spinning light. A bird first, though the wings weren't quite right. Then a flower. When that fell apart, he tried a star, with better success.

"Keyar, how old are you now?"

The star dissipated in a shower of sparkles. "Aunt Ayia, I'm fourteen. You know that."

"I can't keep track. You grow so fast." Or was it just that the shadows were growing in her mind as well as in the corners?

"Not fast enough. It will be seven years before I'm old enough to join the service." Keyar's mouth pulled into a pout, though that wasn't a natural attitude for him, and his normal, serene expression quickly returned.

"You want to join the service? What put that into your head? Your father will never allow it. You understand that, don't you?"

Hodryk, ensnared by shadow, would sooner kill his son than allow him to enter the anti-shadow service. Ayia pushed the thought aside. She didn't believe it. She wouldn't believe it. Surely, death was a line he wouldn't cross. But he would keep Keyar out of the service. That much was certain.

"I'll find a way. It's partly because of Father that I want to join. I owe the Creator. Even more than most people. For not stopping Father." Keyar hesitated, and light scattered out from his fingertips. He showed no awareness of his lack of control. If it was lack of control. Maybe he meant to spew light like glitter. His face took on an earnest frown. "I think, maybe, he's gone to the shadow. No, I'm sure of it. And nothing I've said or done has helped. I don't know what else to do about it. How to help Mother."

Ayia shifted in her rocking chair, letting its motion calm her before she spoke. "Your mother. Does she still spin light?"

Zeezia came from the corner of the room that served as a kitchen, where she had been hovering over a pan of muffins fresh from the oven. She sat on the floor beside Ayia's chair, clutching its arm and slowing its rocking motion.

"She only spins when Father is away," she said. "But not anymore. Not these past seven or eight days. Not since Father caught her and . . ."

"What did he do? Did he beat her again?"

"No." Keyar's voice was harsh, as Ayia had never heard it before. "He threatened her with darkness. It swirled around her. It . . . took her, for a moment. Aunt Ayia, can someone hold a person in shadow stasis the way the medics do with light?"

"I don't know." Ayia suspected she did know, but she buried that truth along with other things. "Is that what you thought was happening?"

"Yes."

"Zeezia, did you see this?"

Zeezia pressed her forehead against Ayia's knee. Ayia had to lean down to hear her muffled voice. "It looked like it. Mother's hardly spoken since that day and doesn't even try to spin light. And Father gets angry more often. With Mother. With Keyar. Sometimes, even with me." She lifted her head. Her eyes were dry, but her lips trembled as she continued. "He's even kept me from going to town for a whole moon cycle."

Ayia hadn't heard this. "You aren't going to the library to study with that scribe anymore?"

"He won't let me. Says my place is at home. But I don't want to stay home and cook and tend the garden and the other things mother's stuck with. I want to study. There's so much to learn, and I've hardly gotten started."

"You have a good mind. There's no limit to what you can become if you're given a chance. Your father used to encourage your studies. Has he given any reason for this change?"

"Just that Master Vesor teaches lies. At least he promised to give me things to read at home and said he'd help me understand them. So, I don't have to quit studying. And he said he'd teach me to spin the way spinning was meant to be done. I think he wants to turn me into a Dark Spinner."

Ayia took a deep breath. Her brother was becoming someone she didn't recognize. He had set out to prove how harmless Dark Spinning was. Just colors and shadows that allowed for more nuance in the spinning of light. He hadn't meant to hurt anyone, his own family, least of all. Fazia had tried to stop him when he first began, but he had just laughed. Now she was too worn down by his abuse to fight back.

Both Zeezia and Keyar were watching her, waiting for an answer, for advice, or at least an assessment of the changes in their father. She searched for something, though she knew she was the wrong person to give what they sought.

She sensed an approaching aura. She recognized it as her brother a moment before a shadow passed across the window and a loud banging broke the silence of waiting. Zeezia scrambled to her feet, trying to smooth her hair and her rumpled tunic at the same time. "It's Father," she whispered. Her eyes were large, and the blue flecks in them swirled erratically.

Ayia looked away. Zeezia's eyes made her dizzy. She concentrated, instead, on Keyar. His eyes swirled a steady pattern, and his expression was set, determined.

Hodryk didn't wait for anyone to answer his knock. He pushed the door open, letting it slam against the wall. Keyar jumped out of the way, his hasty movement drawing his father's attention.

"You!" Hodryk's voice had a hard edge. "Why aren't you about your chores? Did you think I'd do them for you if you ran off to play?"

"No, Father. I did most of them. There's plenty of time to finish the rest before dinner."

"Don't talk back to me, boy. And you, too." His piercing gaze traveled from Zeezia's head down to her bare feet and then flicked away, dismissing her. "Your mother's making preserves. Go help her. At once."

Zeezia sidled across the room, her eyes lowered, her hands tugging at her rumpled clothing. She kept as much distance from her father as possible as she approached the door. Just as she was about to slip past him, Hodryk reached out his arm to block her way. When she stopped, he cupped her chin in his hand and lifted her face toward his. For a moment, his eyes softened.

"If you're a good girl and work hard, we'll read something together after dinner. I found a book I think will interest you, and I can explain anything you don't understand."

He released her. Her lips curved in a half smile. With a quick nod, she slipped out the door and disappeared. Keyar exhaled sharply, a sound of disgust that mimicked someone twice his age.

Hodryk took a step toward him, his hand poised. He appeared more likely to strike his son than to cup his chin in his palm, as he had done with his daughter. His eyes narrowed. "You have a problem with your sister and I reading together? Jealous, perhaps? But you're welcome to join us when your chores are done." His voice was icy.

"I will not read the writings of Chorzon, and you and Zeezia shouldn't either."

Ayia stared at her brother in astonishment. He was reading Chorzon to Zeezia? She shuddered and her stomach churned. She had dipped into Chorzon's essays just once, and despite her fascination with shadows, she had vowed never to read another word. The first Dark Spinner's writings had not only inflamed the better part of a generation and enticed them to start a rebellion against the Creator, but had driven many of his readers mad. Ayia's fingers sparked light, as she tried to drive the memory of those words away.

And Hodryk thought this was appropriate reading for his young daughter? Things were worse than she had feared.

Hodryk glared at Keyar, his hand still raised, threatening, though he didn't touch the boy. "You think you know better than your father, that you can tell me what I should do, and censure my reading for me?" Beneath the ice in Hodryk's voice, there burned a scorching fury.

Keyar stood steadfast, unfazed by his father's acrimony. "Chorzon was a liar. He said whatever would get people to follow him and help him. He didn't care what happened to them. How many died or had their lives ruined?"

"He led them bravely in the cause of freedom."

"And you're leading my sister to freedom?" Keyar's voice was heavy with scorn.

"Yes. Freedom. I would lead you too, if you would give up your foolish notions and open your mind."

"Never." Keyar spoke with vehemence and favored his father with a long, hard stare, neither backing down nor breaking eye contact. In the end, it was Hodryk who averted his gaze. Keyar gave a small nod and walked out of the house with a firm step.

Unable to cow his son, Hodryk turned his ire on Ayia. "Why are you hiding my children from me here? What right do you have?"

Ayia kept her chair moving, let her hands rest unflinching on its arms. "I wasn't hiding them. I invited them because I haven't seen them for a long time. They are my closest family. Is it surprising I would want to spend a little time with them?"

Hodryk let his gaze roam over the room, his lips curling as he took in the small space that served as kitchen, pantry, dining room, and gathering area. Shadows swirled around the tips of his fingers and crawled toward his arms, and Ayia instinctively shuttered any shadows she had gathered in the corners of the space.

He turned his gaze back to her and smirked, though his eyes remained hard, with angry scarlet flecks swirling against the yellow of his irises. "You've no excuse for trying to steal my children's loyalty. You could very well have had children of your own. You could be living somewhere decent, instead of this tiny hovel."

"This hovel, as you call it, suits my needs."

"I daresay. Wouldn't Bryton howl with laughter if he saw you now? I hear he has a mansion on Exalton and two dozen human servants." He leaned closer. "But not married yet, if messages be true. And I know you still keep his likeness." She felt her eyes widen, and he grinned. "Yes, I've seen it."

"Then you've been snooping where you have no business."

"It's my business if I think you're hiding things for my children. Books I've forbidden have gone missing, and this seemed as likely a hiding place as any."

"But you didn't find them. I'm not hiding things for your children."

"Not this time, not so I've found, anyway." He flicked his gaze around the room, letting it rest on kitchen items, a row of books on a shelf in one corner, a vase of flowers on the table. "Won't let up my guard, though." He paused, and the corners of his mouth lifted in a rare shadow of his old smile. "Might trust you more if you'd show some interest in Exalton. Why don't you plan to go with us, myself and the children you're so fond of? I'll send a message to Bryton for you, if you like."

Ayia's heart pounded, but she forced her breathing to stay calm and even. It would never do to let Hodryk know he had rattled her. "Why would you be sending and receiving messages from Exalton? It's a forbidden world."

Hodryk threw back his head and laughed as he turned toward the door. With his hand on the latch, he threw a glance back her way. "No more forbidden than it was when you and I set foot on it twenty years ago. It's only forbidden to those who insist on following the foolish rules of the Light Spinners. They can't stop anyone from coming and going. I've finally wised up and got myself connected. I'd have headed off into the void by now, to set up a new life on a better world, if it weren't for my children. Would prefer to take them with me when I go."

"They won't go with you."

His face darkened to a scowl. "They're hesitant, it's true, Keyar especially, but they'll come around." He paused and caught her eyes with his piercing gaze. The swooping swirls in his eyes sickened her. She wanted to look away but could not.

"You know, it could be a lot less painful," he continued. "They'd come around in a moon cycle or less if you took them in hand. Showed them what color and shadow can do." He raised his eyebrows in a question. "You do understand that, don't you? I've seen the signs. You can't hide it from me."

"That's none of your business. You got what you came for. Now get out."

He didn't argue. She was still as strong as he was, her skills still honed, even twenty-five years after her first training. He knew that. She had made sure of it, training where he would see her often enough to leave no doubt. She lifted one hand from the chair, curled her fingers, and let the hilt of a light sword begin to form. If a little shadow was mixed in with the light, he wouldn't be able to see it.

His eyes flicked to her hand and back to her face. Good. He was uncertain. She waited, not forming the sword but not letting its hilt dissipate, either. After a moment, he drew a deep breath and tromped out of the door, slamming it behind him.

She waited until the sound of his footsteps faded away, then she looked at the sword hilt in her hand. Doubt crept into her mind, fed by the shadows that were slinking back into the corners of the room. She took a deep breath and let the sword form.

Her gaze traveled its length to the bright tip more than an arms-length from her hand. She studied it with an experienced eye. The tip was bright, sparkling as any light sword should, but along its length, its light was not true. Though no discernable black streaks swirled around or through the blade, yet it was dull, sullied. Concentrating, she cleared the impurities. For a moment, the sword shone bright, as it had many years ago when she was an eager young agent, on Merdoma for her first assignment.

But she couldn't hold its purity. It dimmed, and she let it dissipate with a sigh. The shadows were becoming stronger. Soon it would be all she knew.

But not yet. Not today. The sun was still high in the sky. She would seek its light, since she had failed to spin her own light. She rose from the chair and went to the tiny bedroom to tie her hair out of the way for gardening. She paused in front of the clothes chest, her hand going to the handle of the top drawer before she realized what she was doing.

She snatched it back and stared at the drawer, then slowly reached for the handle and pulled it open. Her fingers groped around the back of the drawer, beneath her clean underclothes, until they found the hard, smooth rectangle there and pulled it out. Bryton's face stared up at her from the old light-etching.

The artist had caught the exact likeness of his laughing mouth and the joking twinkle in his eye. The etching held no colors, but Ayia's imagination filled them in: pale green hair, flecks of a more vivid green swirling in his blue eyes, skin almost as dark as that of the Sal-Enos from constant sun exposure. And she heard his voice again, laughing one moment, barking commands to the trainees under his tutelage the next, and then whispering tender nothings in her ear.

She shoved the etching back under her clothes and slammed the drawer shut. She snatched her hat from the peg by the door, jammed it on her head, and strode out to the garden. Her agitation frightened the chezoks, who ran bleating from her, the two babies scampering to stay close to their mothers. The chickens in the yard also scurried out of her way as she headed for the shed and flung its door wide.

She grabbed a hoe and attacked the weeds in the garden, looking for distraction. Just that. Peace would be too much to ask for, but she would need to calm down before milking time or the chezoks would never let her near them. She hoed at a frenzied pace until the sun dipped toward the horizon, when, finally, the softer light and physical exertion did their work and she was able to straighten and take a deep, calming breath.

Bryton was history. It had taken only one secret visit to Exalton to convince her she wanted no part of that world. He had laughed at her, seeming unaffected by the swirling shadows and the dark atmosphere of the landscape. He overlaid everything with his own bright outlook, his constant laughter, his ready jokes. But it had taken her years to shake the impression of corruption from that one visit. She had no desire to go back.

Leaning on her hoe, she studied her small place. She could have done anything after she resigned from the service. Her skills were many and varied. Or she might have married. Not Bryton. But Quenlin had fancied her. Fancied her still. And he was a good man, always looking for a way to help her. Always keeping an eye on the children for her when she could not.

But she had put him off. This small life, the life of a subsistence farmer, suited her. It gave her time to think, to explore ideas. And it had given her the privacy to explore the shadows. She had needed to understand what drew Bryton. Had needed to understand what she had rejected.

But now, too late, she saw what a mistake it had been to hide out here. Better to have moved on and fashioned a useful life, occupying her mind with light-filled pursuits. Or, at the very least, better to have lived closer to neighbors, who would have caught her at her experiments and stopped her long ago. Now the tendrils of shadow wrapped themselves around her small house and swirled in front of her feet as she paced about her garden or tended the animals. They menaced her from the dark trees pressing all around her property, and when she fled from the trees, seeking refuge inside the house, they mocked her from the corners.

She was still able to hold them at bay for a short period of time if a neighbor dropped by or when Zeezia and Keyar came for a visit. But for how much longer? And what would she do when she saw in the children's faces that they had guessed the truth? Zeezia's swirling eyes she might be able to ignore by simply looking away. But Keyar? She could never bear to receive from him the uncompromising stare he had favored his father with this afternoon.

She worked outside until dusk deepened so she could no longer see what she was doing and evening rains moved from mist to drizzle, soaking her tunic. When she returned to the house, she built up the fire and lit every lamp she owned. She prepared a simple dinner and browsed her book shelf for something to read while she ate, hoping to disrupt unwanted reminiscence. She settled on an old childhood favorite. As she slid the book from its spot, something fell with a dull thud at the back of the shelf. There was a book there, one she didn't recognize.

It was small, hide bound, and dyed a beautiful green and gold. It fell open in her hand to reveal a flowing script that danced across the page. Setting down her childhood storybook, she flipped to the title page of the strange volume, breathing in the earthy smell of the old book with appreciation. *The Founding of the Service*, she read. *Philosophy and Function.* The next page was scribed with the oath all agents took at the end of their training, binding them to the Creator's service for the rest of their lives. The oath she had taken once. The oath Hodryk and Bryton had also taken.

She sat down at the table, with her dinner in front of her and the little book resting to one side. She reached for her food, but her fingers found the edges of the book's binding instead, and caressed them. Inside the front cover, she saw her brother's name, not inked there, but etched in his great, pompous light script. She smiled. Keyar had spent some time at the bookcase when he first arrived earlier in the day. Hodryk was clever, but his son might be his match.

Ayia read the little book as she ate and continued after her plate was empty, starting with the oath and working her way into the philosophical essays.

She stopped reading only long enough to drop her dirty dishes into the washtub, adjust the lamps, and move to her rocking chair. She read for hours, letting the words hold the shadows at bay. A world rested within them, a world she had disavowed but now yearned toward with deep regret. She read until she fell asleep, and in her dreams, when they came, the shadows that had filled her dreams of late were lanced with light.

She jerked awake to the sound of pounding on her door. She stared at the door, bewildered, the realization that someone was on the other side working its slow way into her sleep-fogged brain. Her gaze darted to the timepiece on the mantel. Half the sand had slipped through the funnel. Who could be at the door with the night half gone?

The pounding came again, louder, faster. Ayia needed to answer. As she stood, the little book tumbled from her lap to the floor. Suddenly wary, she scooped it up and tucked it into her waistband at her back, pulling her tunic over it before moving toward the door.

As she drew near, she remembered to test the aura of whoever was on the other side. Expecting Hodryk, what she sensed surprised her. She jerked the door open and Zeezia and Keyar tumbled in, a mass of arms and legs, across her threshold.

Keyar disentangled himself from his sister and grabbed the edge of the door, slamming it shut. "Quick, you have to hide us, Aunt Ayia. I tried to lay a false trail, but Father will figure it out soon."

"What's happened?" Ayia asked as she helped Zeezia to her feet.

Zeezia threw her arms around Ayia and buried her face in Ayia's shoulder. "He got angry and Mother tried to . . . she tried . . . and he swirled, and . . . and Keyar spun me away before I could ask him why or calm him down." Sobs, building into a torrent, made any further words incoherent.

"What did he do?" Ayia asked Keyar, as she patted Zeezia's wet hair. "Where is Fazia? Where is your mother?"

"Dead." Keyar's voice was like granite from the deep quarries on the far side of Luxera. Heavy. Unyielding. Asking nothing and expecting nothing.

"What happened?"

"She tried to resist Father. When he called Zeezia to read with him, she tried to stop them. They argued like I've never heard before. She started to spin light, but he filled her with his shadow and then strangled her with his bare hands. He would have killed us too, if I hadn't spun us away before he got to us."

Zeezia lifted her head. "He wouldn't have killed me." Her words hung in the air as she dropped her head back to Ayia's shoulder.

Ayia shook her head. This couldn't be true. Hodryk loved Fazia. He had pursued her for years before winning her hand, and he had never been happier than the day they were joined. Keyar was watching her, reading her, reading the doubt in her face.

"Believe me, Aunt Ayia. Father is dark and evil. He said he was taking us to Exalton. Taking Zeezia and me. I would never have gone with him. But. . .he got a hold on Zeezia, and Mother attacked him. She gave herself so we could get away. Now it's my duty to keep Zeezia safe. But . . ." His voice cracked and his eyes softened with his uncertainty. "I don't know what to do. Where to hide. Where can we go that he can't find us? He'll feel our auras, and he won't stop until he has us. And I'm too tired to spin anymore."

"Shh. Let me think."

Ayia reached out as far as she could, searching for other auras. For one aura in particular. There was no one nearby, but she sensed something on the edges of her perception. He would be here before long, but there might be time to get out of the house before he came.

It would be a long walk to get anywhere that might offer safety. Spinning would be faster, but she couldn't spin both children. Keyar would try to help, but his face was haggard with his exhaustion. And Zeezia watched her with a blank expression. She'd get no help there. Besides, Hodryk would sense any spinning and make a short chase of it.

She didn't dare expose the few neighbors in the area to Hodryk's anger. The one exception might be Quenlin. But it would take several hours, all that remained of the night, even to get to his place. She'd need supplies. The children had come with nothing, and from their haggard appearance and tattered clothing, she guessed they had been running, spinning and running, for hours.

She poured some water from her jug and made them drink, then gave each of them a handful of grain wafers. She wrapped more wafers in a napkin and thrust them into her tunic pocket and found her clay canteen, the one she carried when she went tramping among the trees. She filled it with water, but after that, her mind refused to focus any longer. There must be more she should do, more that they would need. But no. Anything more would just slow them down.

Keyar pushed past her into the kitchen area and grabbed a small knife, which he stuck in his boot.

Then he pulled two of Ayia's shawls off the hook by the door—shawls for sitting outside watching the stars on a pleasantly cool, dry evening. The type of evening she could barely imagine at this moment.

Keyar handed one shawl to Ayia and wrapped the other around Zeezia's shoulders. Zeezia still stood beside the door, the empty cup in her hand, dripping from the rain and shivering. Dropping the cup, she pulled the shawl close and held it with hands tucked inside. Ayia berated herself. She hadn't even noticed Zeezia was wet and cold.

"Where will we go?" Keyar asked, his hand on the door handle.

"We'll see. I have a couple of ideas." Ayia hesitated to commit herself to any course of action just yet. "The first thing is to get far enough away from here before your father comes, so he can't feel our auras. Or at least not enough to be sure where we are. We'll walk as fast as we can." She saw the protesting pucker between Zeezia's eyes. "No, I won't spin you. We're trying to hide, not broadcast our location."

She bolted the house's one door. "That should slow him a little. He might assume I'm sleeping."

She snuffed out the lamps and helped the children climb from her bedroom window. They slid from the window down into a bed of thick heather that sprang back with a burst of dusky fragrance after they stepped away, hiding any signs of their passage. The area beyond the heather-bed was hard packed and filled with the prints of chezoks and chickens, as well as her own footprints, left here daily as she cared for her animals. Even if Hodryk came after sunup and examined her yard, he would be unable to tell which direction they had gone, or even that the children had been here. The slight drizzle finished the work, churning the prints into mucky confusion.

She led them away from her house and into the thickest part of the forest. The rain abated, and the clouds rolled back enough to reveal a scattering of stars, but it was still a very dark night. Keyar flicked light from his fingers until he gathered enough control to form a small light disk, but Ayia frowned at him and shook her head, warning him against the telltale light. He let the disk die, and she motioned both children to follow close behind her. She guided them by memory, by her deep, expansive knowledge of these woods. She had tramped here for fifteen years and knew every tree and stone.

Keyar followed her with a trusting, confident step. Zeezia was less sure. She stumbled over every small stone or exposed tree root and clutched alternately at Ayia or Keyar, slowing them all. They were not making fast enough progress. Ayia should have been too far away to sense Hodryk's aura as he approached her house, yet awareness of him, of his methodical examination of the area, infiltrated her mind with fearful clarity. And if she could detect him, he would recognize her as well, if he thought to test for her presence.

Her bolted door slowed him some, and then he had to puzzle out where she had gone and whether his children were with her. She perceived these things vaguely, along with his brooding anger, as she struggled to increase her distance from him. His ability to identify others' auras had a wide range, and she must be sure they were beyond it before he attempted to follow them into the woods. She pushed Zeezia ahead of her, confident Keyar would stay close behind.

Slowly, Ayia's sense of Hodryk's aura dissipated, but not knowing where he was and where he might appear next was worse than knowing he was behind her. Her shoulders and chest tensed and she struggled for a deep breath.

She tried to boost their speed, but Zeezia stumbled and cried and wouldn't be hurried. Even Keyar fell behind, though he never complained. Ayia reminded herself that they had been through trauma, through flight, through fear, and without sleep, and she tried to be gentle with them. They were almost to Quenlin's sturdy, substantial house. He was a strong Light Spinner. They would be safe there, at least until they could make better plans.

They approached the house warily, avoiding the road and skirting to the back, where a wide veranda led to the kitchen. All was dark and silent. Quenlin was not an early riser. Ayia would have to rouse him without making so much noise that she alerted his near neighbors, who already had a lamp shining in one window.

Ayia tapped lightly on the back door. When that brought no response, she scooted around to tap on the window that would open to Quenlin's bedroom. When Quenlin still didn't respond, she made a fist and prepared to pound, but a hand caught her wrist before she could land the first blow.

She jumped and stifled an exclamation.

"Shh." Keyar's voice came to her in a whisper. "What are you trying to do?"

"Rouse Quenlin and ask him to help us."

"I don't think he's here."

"How would you know that?"

"He came by to check on us yesterday. No, the day before. Told Mother he was going into Luxa City for a council meeting yesterday. Wouldn't be back until late, or probably he'd just stay in the city overnight and come home in the morning."

Ayia stifled a curse, then frowned. The expression she had almost spat out was one she'd picked up from Bryton all those years ago. Why had it come to mind now? It was a loathsome word, filled with darkness, a word she did not want the children to hear, especially from her lips.

"What do we do now?" Zeezia's voice was too loud, her question ending in a whine.

"We keep going." Ayia whispered.

"Can't we go inside? Quenlin won't care." Zeezia's voice was still too loud. She had her hand on the door latch.

Ayia put her finger to her lips and shook her head. "Your father will look for us here soon. Without Quenlin's help, we won't be any better off than at my house."

"Can't you protect us?" Keyar kept his voice low, but it had as insistent an edge as his sister's. "You were an agent once."

"That was a long time ago. I haven't spun much light lately." Her shadow sword might be a match for Hodryk's, but that was something she hoped Keyar and Zeezia would never see. "We keep going."

"Where?" Keyar asked.

Exhausted and afraid, both of them. Ayia wasn't as tired as they were, but she was tired enough. And afraid. And not just of her brother. With each step she took it got harder to hold the shadows at bay. Only the knowledge that Hodryk would find her the instant she spun shadow helped shore up her determination and will, but it wouldn't work forever. And now there was only one place she could go to keep the children safe. A place where any shadow she accidentally spun might land her in Yellaz prison.

"We'll go to the city. We're more than halfway already. There will be people there who can help us. Come on."

Keyar hesitated, standing poised between Ayia and Zeezia, as if torn between the two choices they offered him. "It's so far, Aunt Ayia. Can't we rest here first?"

"And let your father catch up to us?"

"Maybe Quenlin will come."

"Maybe, but we can't count on him being in time. We keep going. When we get to the city, you can rest."

Keyar hesitated only a moment longer before nodding. He reached his hand out for Zeezia. "Come on. I'll help you."

Zeezia held tight to the door latch. "I don't want to. I don't care if Father catches us. Just let me rest."

Ayia peered at Zeezia, trying to read her expression. Though the night was graying toward dawn, it was still too dark to see her face clearly, to gage how deep her weariness, how eroded her will to continue.

"You don't mean that," she said softly. "Your father killed your mother. There's no way to know what he'll do when he finds you."

"He won't hurt me. Father would never hurt me."

"Maybe not. But I would never have believed he would hurt Fazia either. He loved her so much. I can't take that chance with you. Take Keyar's hand. I'll go slower until it gets a little lighter and we can see better."

Little by little, Ayia and Keyar coaxed Zeezia away from the door and back among the trees. Ayia was tempted to walk on the road. It ran smooth and straight all the way from Quenlin's house to the steps of the Service Administration Building in Luxa City. It would be easier and faster than tramping through the woods.

But it would also be easier for Hodryk. He would have no trouble catching them well before they reached the city's outskirts, and the only people around to help them would be innocent travelers who might get hurt. If there were other reasons for Ayia to avoid a road that would soon be filled with people, she buried them, along with the shadows that threatened to flow back into her mind whenever she let her guard down.

Their pace was painfully slow now, and they had walked little more than another hour when Ayia sensed her brother's unmistakable aura again. Her path through the woods and fields slowed him down a bit, but not as much as it slowed her and the children. And as the predawn light grew stronger and the open fields more numerous, her tension increased. She expected at any moment to hear a shout or other sounds of pursuit that would tell her Hodryk had sighted them.

She took her bearings in the next open space. The road was not far off, the line of it visible, brown and grey, against the backdrop of Luxera's lush vegetation. It was beginning to fill with early travelers—farmers with loads to get to market, people heading to Luxa City to shop or conduct business, and folks out for a leisurely stroll. Anyone with a need for speed and without a heavy load would spin to their destination, but this road was a pleasant path for those who had no need, or wish, for hurry.

The land surrounding Luxa City was a beautiful, productive region filled with fields, pastures, orchards, and vineyards. Ayia usually enjoyed coming this way and often walked to the outskirts of the city, even after she became reluctant to visit the city itself.

But she had never seen this landscape as she saw it today in the faint but growing light, as the sun fought its way up through the clouds in the east. Its muted rays cast shadows from each barn, from every Zanna tree and every vine, from each stalk of ripening grain in the fields, even from individual blades of grass. These dark splotches of shade on the ground lingered like a curse, menacing, suggesting treachery and death.

To keep the children hidden, Ayia needed to lead them into the shelter of the trees. But as they passed through the first orchard, and the shadowed way whispered to her with the voices of thousands of tiny leaves, she shuddered and looked for the nearest way of escape. She burst out into the open track between groves of trees with a gasp, shaking violently. The children followed far behind, struggling to catch up.

She stopped, berating herself for her cowardice. For her niece and nephew she would do anything. Even stifle her fear. Only clear thinking offered hope of escape. Clear thinking. No fear. Clear thinking. No fear.

But though Ayia muttered these words over and over while she waited for Keyar and Zeezia to catch their breaths, and again as they started through the next stand of trees, neither her heart nor her mind would listen. The shadows would catch her. It was too late to run from them. They occupied her mind and permeated the world around her.

The orchards ended at last. Ayia charged into the vast space of a glowing pasture. The sun topped the low edge of clouds on the eastern horizon, and its light splashed over waving grasses and the brilliant hues of wildflowers. In her mad dash to be away from the trees, Ayia reached the middle of the pasture before the beauty of the morning checked her flight.

She stopped abruptly, with the awareness of light, as she had never known it before. As it intensified, it sought out the dark places and illuminated them. Even the shadows cast by the trees, both behind and beyond her, seemed only gradations of the light. There was only one place the light did not touch. Even as her entire being yearned for it, darkness raged within her and she could no longer hold it back.

She held out her hand to form a sword, as if that might help her combat the darkness. Tendrils of shadow wreathed her hand, forming the sword's hilt. The hilt undulated as she fought to purify the murky gloom from it, fought to pull the light from the world around her into herself and her spinning construct.

"Aunt Ayia . . ." Keyar's voice, hushed though it was, held an edge of shock and accusation.

Ayia tore her eyes from the sword hilt, but she wouldn't look at Keyar's face. She sought a place to rest her gaze anywhere but on him. She looked to her other side and found Zeezia. The flecks in

Zeezia's eyes swirled madly, but as Ayia watched, the swirls slowed and recognition dawned.

"Father was right." Zeezia's face was calm, set.

Right about what? Ayia looked away, fought to dispel the shadows. Fought to draw the light back into her being. But as she struggled, a greater darkness fell over her mind. An aura accosted her, so familiar she would know it no matter where in the seven worlds it came to her. An aura known to her from the cradle. It commanded her, and she realized Hodryk had been waiting years for her to reveal herself, even as he alternately bullied and scorned her and left her alone in her self-imposed isolation.

He emerged from the orchard, coming for her as much as he came for his children. She doubted she still had the power to resist him. Inky tendrils wrapped themselves around her legs and rose, reaching for her waist. Her breath came in short gasps as she fought, fought for Keyar and Zeezia, though she no longer had hope for herself. If her only weapon was a sword of dark shadow, she would use that against her brother and give his children a chance to escape.

A dark blade stretched up from the hilt in her hands, growing until it was her preferred length, balanced perfectly for her strength and fighting style. Her mind accepted its dark shimmer, gloried in it even, though a part of her still resisted it.

Hodryk stopped at a distance of fifty paces and watched her, a knowing smile on his face.

"There you are," he called. "Now that you've finally admitted your true nature, it's time to come with me. Bring my children to me, and we'll go together to a place where you can spin without fear. Darkness, light, color. Whatever you wish. Come, sister dear. You've been moving this way for a long time. I've seen it, even when you have not. It's time to embrace the choices you've already made and come with me to Exalton. And my sweet daughter. Come. And you, too, son of my body. Come to freedom and peace. But we must go now, before that insufferable cad can interfere."

Beside her, Keyar took in a sharp breath. "Quenlin," he said in a low voice, for her ears alone.

The spin of the dark sword faltered. Ayia risked a glance at Keyar. His face was turned away from her, turned toward the distant road, toward a shining figure that had detached itself from the thoroughfare and advanced in their direction with adamant stride.

Quenlin, on his way home from Luxa City. Quenlin, who was always attuned to her aura, even though she continually rejected him. Quenlin, whose light was strong and pure. She would have cried with relief, but she knew he was too late. Not too late for the children, but too late for her. Soon the shadows would have complete sway over her mind, and though her eyes would see his light, her heart and her soul would not.

Even so, his approach gave her the strength to resist Hodryk.

"I will never come with you," she shouted, glad for the defiance in her voice that hid her despair.

Zeezia huffed loudly. "Speak for yourself. I want my father." She straightened, exhaustion pushed aside by resolve.

"Zeezia, no." Ayia searched for words that would have power to hold the girl back. "He'll take you to Exalton. He'll turn you into a Dark Spinner. Once you go, you won't be able to turn back. That isn't what your mother would have wanted for you."

Zeezia hesitated. She had loved her mother. A shadow of grief flitted across her face, but she banished it at once. "Don't tell me what to do, Aunt Ayia. I've always listened to you, but you've lied to me." She gave the shadows swirling around Ayia's legs and torso a meaningful glance. "At least Father has never lied. With him I can study and become whatever I decide. He'll give me that. What can you offer?"

Ayia had no answer. She had nothing to offer but a knowledge of light and shadow that Zeezia was not prepared to understand.

Zeezia walked toward her father. Hodryk waited for her, arms outstretched.

"No. Don't go." Keyar's plea was a clarion call. Zeezia's steps faltered, and Ayia's heart skipped a beat as hope surged. She didn't have anything to offer, but Keyar did. His aura was pure and unsullied. He had a right to call his sister back.

But after that one misstep, Zeezia steadied her stride and kept moving forward toward Hodryk. She did not look back at her brother.

Ayia searched for Quenlin. He was her last hope. But he didn't seem to understand the need for haste. Ayia guessed he was still close to two hundred paces away, and though he had formed a light sword, he did not quicken his steps, nor did he show any sign of translating to a spin.

Keyar's eyes tracked her gaze. They flicked from Quenlin to Hodryk, gaging the distance between them, and then to Zeezia, who was now only twenty-five paces from her father. He formed the hilt of a light sword in one hand, but the blade he pushed out from his hilt wobbled, and he couldn't hold its form.

Zeezia was twenty paces from Hodryk. Shadow wreathed Hodryk's legs in the beginnings of a dark spin. He would be ready for a transit into the void as soon as Zeezia reached him.

Keyar let the sword dissipate and tried light disks. They formed perfectly in his hands, but when he tried to release them, they sputtered and fell apart in a shower of sparkles. He gave a low cry, reaching for them, then let them go.

Zeezia was fifteen paces from Hodryk. Keyar gave Ayia a quick, sidelong glance, then bent and pulled her kitchen knife from his boot. He gripped the blade in his right hand, blunt side against his palm, and stepped forward lightly on his right foot, his form perfect for throwing. He rocked onto his back foot and tested his grip on the blade, then turned his face toward his father.

Ayia stared at him. Where had he learned this? She had no doubt in that moment that he would hit his target. And he would have his father's blood on his hands for the rest of his life. She let her dark sword dissipate and leaped for his arm, pushing him over and knocking the blade from his hand. He harrumphed loudly as he hit the ground, and then scrabbled for the knife, but Ayia was quicker.

The blade of the knife fit into her palm like a familiar friend. She had chopped and diced with it for many years, but it had been a while since she had thrown a knife. A sword would be a more effective weapon for her, but one look at Zeezia confirmed that there was no time for a sword. She was less than ten paces from her father. A few more steps and she would block Ayia's site line.

Ayia relaxed, taking a deep breath, and let the instinct of years of training take over. The knife flew from her fingers and buried itself in Hodryk's left shoulder. As Zeezia reached him, he fell, spurting a shower of blood.

Zeezia screamed. She fell to her knees beside him and placed her hand over the knife embedded in his flesh. Blood pulsed out in a steady rhythm. She snatched her hand away and stared at the dark smear across her palm.

Keyar regained his feet and started toward her at a run, but when she saw him, Zeezia sprang to her feet and pushed her bloody hand toward him, palm out, in a gestured command to stop.

"Stay away. You've killed him."

Keyar stopped at her command, but leaned toward her, as if to get as close as possible, as close as she would allow. "I didn't. Is he dead?"

"I don't know. He's dying, at least. And it's as much your fault as Aunt Ayia's."

"He killed our mother. I couldn't let him take you."

"Mother shouldn't have interfered with him. And neither should you. This wasn't your choice. It was mine, and I'm still making it."

"Zeezia, what are you thinking?" Keyar's voice cracked, and he took a step toward her.

"Stop. Don't come any closer. I'm going to do what he wanted me to do. I'm going to Exalton."

"No, don't, please. How can you get there alone?"

"How else, silly boy? I'm going to spin."

Ayia felt someone move up beside her and touch her elbow. She caught the shine of Quenlin's sword before he let it dissipate.

"What can I do?" he asked.

"We've got to stop her. She doesn't understand what she's saying," Ayia started toward Zeezia as she spoke. She heard the rustle of grasses behind her as Quenlin followed her.

Zeezia saw them coming and scurried to the far side of Hodryk's prostrate form, as if to gain protection from him.

"Don't come any closer." Her voice was shrill. "You killed him. I don't want you near. You killed him and you lied to me. Get away. Get away."

Zeezia gestured wildly with her hands, but Ayia kept moving forward, one careful step after another. She passed Keyar. Just a few more steps.

"No," Zeezia wailed. "I won't let you. Don't touch me." She leaned down and touched her father with her bloody hand, leaving a rust-red smear across his forehead. "I'll do what you wanted, Father. I'm sorry I didn't listen better, but I'll do it now."

Ayia took another step. Zeezia was little more than an arm's length away. But as Ayia reached out to grab her, Zeezia began to swirl, to spin.

She spun light. It's what she had been trained to do. But she tried to spin shadow, and tendrils, like smoke, wound themselves within the swirl of her light. Too late, Ayia started her own spin, a spin more shadow than light. But before she could complete the translation, Zeezia pushed away. She headed straight up, into the void.

Ayia's half-formed heart thumped madly, and she lost her spin. Her feet rested tenuously on the ground, as if they didn't know how to hold her up, and her knees crumpled beneath her. She caught herself with her hands as she fell, and twisted her shoulders and neck around and up, struggling for a glimpse of Zeezia, begging her silently to give it up, to come down. But there was nothing to see. Zeezia had already entered the void.

"She isn't fueled," Ayia said, hearing her voice pitch toward a wail but unable to stop it. "And she doesn't know the way."

Keyar stood beside her, his head tilted back as he, too, searched the sky for a sign of his sister. After a moment, he drew in a deep breath and squared his shoulders. "I'll go get her. I always was faster than her."

He started a spin, but Quenlin's hand on his shoulder stopped him.

"No," Quenlin said. "You'll be lost, too. I'll go."

Keyar tried to squirm away, but Quenlin held him in a firm grip. As Quenlin translated to light, he finally released Keyar. He narrowly avoided pulling the boy into his spin as he shot into the void. Keyar, left on the ground, sparked with the residue of Quenlin's light. Together, Ayia and Keyar watched Quenlin follow Zeezia's trajectory into the void. And kept watching after he had disappeared—waiting and hoping.

Streaks of brilliance flashing across Ayia's vision brought her back to an awareness of herself. Tendrils of shadow still swirled about her hands and arms, making her an easy mark for agents rushing from service headquarters in Luxa City to investigate the Dark Spinning. Mustering all her will power, her face averted from Keyar so she wouldn't know if he watched her, Ayia pushed against shadow until she banished the last of it.

She was clean, spinning neither light nor dark, by the time the first agents finished coalescing, though she might not be able to hold the shadows at bay for long. One agent knelt beside Hodryk, feeling for a pulse. After a moment he leaned back and gestured at another agent, his voice urgent when he spoke.

"Light stasis, now."

A woman agent came to Hodryk's side and enveloped him in spinning light.

Keyar clutched Ayia's arm. "Is he alive?"

The first agent stood and studied Keyar. "Do you know this man?"

"Yes. He's Hodryk. My father. And a Dark Spinner."

The agent shot Ayia a questioning glance. "Can you confirm that? Both the identification and the designation of DS?"

"Yes." Ayia hoped her deep discomfort didn't show in her voice. Who was she to confirm Hodryk's criminal status? But Keyar had named him, and she wouldn't let Keyar down. She waited for him to tell the agent she had been spinning shadow as well, but he kept silent.

The agent nodded and turned his gaze back toward Hodryk. "We felt him. He's a strong spinner. I feared we might have difficulty restraining him, but what fancy tactics can't do, sometimes a simple kitchen knife can."

"Will he live?" Keyar asked in a voice edged with a quaver.

"Too soon to tell, but I suspect he has a chance if he hasn't lost too much blood. The wound isn't deep or dangerous. However, his living will be done at Yellaz prison from now on. He might prefer to have died a free man. But we detected another, weaker dark aura. Who was that?"

Ayia's heart fluttered. Here it was. She couldn't hide any longer. Keyar knew the truth, and would surely not give her more latitude than his own father. His hold on her arm tightened, and she braced, trying to breathe deeply of the sweet morning air and take in every sight and sound all at once, to prepare herself for the thick walls of Yellaz prison.

"My sister," she heard Keyar answer, though it took time for her to make sense of what he said. "She was going to follow our father to Exalton. When he was wounded, she decided to go alone, but. . ." He paused and bit his lip, casting a nervous glance toward the sky. "I don't think she knows how to get there, and she's not a strong spinner. I don't think she can make it."

"How long ago did she transit?" the officer asked, his voice sharp.

"It was just before you came."

"Right. I'll send someone after her, though you understand it might be too late." As he spoke, he motioned several agents closer.

"Quenlin went already."

The officer's eyebrows shot up. "Quenlin! Councilman Quenlin? Well then, there might be a chance. But I'll send agents up, in case he needs help." He motioned toward his agents, and in a flash of light they shot into the void.

Before there was time for them to have done more than clear Luxera's atmosphere, another light broke through from the void and hurtled toward them. It struck the earth hard behind Ayia and Keyar, scattering sparks. As they turned toward that spot, Quenlin coalesced, resuming physical form. He collapsed to his knees, burdened by the weight of Zeezia, who hung limp in his arms.

He turned her and his hands went to her neck, checking for a pulse, and then he sagged, barely retaining his grasp on her.

"Quenlin?" Keyar's voice was small, carrying the despair of a boy who was finally, completely bereft of family.

"She was on the wrong trajectory and burning too fast, too hot, but she wouldn't let me get close. I tried. I just couldn't . . . she panicked and tried to elude me. I'm sorry. I was too slow, too gentle, trying to coax her close. She ran from me, and then she started to coalesce, and I knew. . ."

Tears streamed down his face. Keyar let loose of Ayia's arm and slid to his knees beside Quenlin, reaching for Zeezia's limp hand. Together, the two of them, man and boy, smoothed her rumpled tunic and brushed the hair from her forehead. They touched her with tenderness, ignoring the dark blotches that indicated ruptured blood vessels beneath her skin.

Ayia stood a few paces from them trying to breathe. She averted her gaze from the limp girl and the two mourners and let it roam over the surrounding scene. A team of Light Spinners transited Hodryk away while the remaining agents and officers huddled in conference. It all carried an illusory quality, as if part of a dream or a light spun spectacle.

She pulled her gaze away from this solid yet vague world around her, turned it inward. She found Zeezia's face there, not pale and splotched with death, but vibrant, excited about a book in her hand. Ayia tried to see what her imaginary Zeezia was reading. It was a colorful volume, filled with light etchings that came to life as Ayia examined them--scenes of a joyful childhood, of the warmth of close family life, of a master scribe who opened the worlds of history and philosophy and literature to Zeezia. Ayia caught glimpses of her own face among those pages, happy now and then, and sending loving glances toward her niece, but growing darker as the pages of the book turned.

Tendrils of shadow rose from the pages, and then Zeezia stared out of one of the last filled pages, startling in the clarity of her features, brows drawn together and mouth pulled into a frown of anger as she shouted "You lied to me. You're worse than Father. He never lied to me."

The book flew out of Zeezia's hand, and the remaining pages, so many pages, all blank, riffled, as by a great wind, for an instant. Then the book slammed shut, stilling them. Ayia shut her eyes and the image dissipated, but the words the imagined Zeezia had shouted, the same words the real Zeezia had spoken just a short while earlier, rang in her mind.

Cautiously, she opened her eyes and looked around. Most of the agents had gone. A few, along with the lead officer, gathered around Quenlin and Keyar. No one paid any attention to Ayia. She couldn't see Keyar's face. She wanted to see it, even though she wouldn't like what she saw there.

He was perceptive. It wouldn't take him long to remember Zeezia's words, to remember the darkness that had prompted them, and its source. He would remember that Ayia had spun shadow in his presence, and he would name her to the authorities. Dark Spinner.

Ayia would not flee or fight when they came to arrest her. She would not contest the verdict. She would honor Keyar by letting his testimony about her stand uncontested. But until they came, she would savor every borrowed moment of freedom, every breath of fresh air, every scent from the verdant Luxeran landscape.

It was not yet noon, and a fine day for hiking. She turned away and walked quietly across the field and into the shade of the trees, tense as she waited for someone to shout her name, to call her back.

But the shout didn't come, and she kept walking. She walked for hours, without eating, without drinking. As the shadows slanted toward day's end, she reached her house. Exhausted, weak, her throat parched and aching, she stepped through the door that Hodryk had left open the night before and collapsed into her rocking chair.

She sat in a stupor, letting the silence wash over her, feeling a great emptiness that precluded even the shadows she had been so drawn to only a day ago. She sat there until the faint sound of bleating reached her ears, reminding her that her chezoks had missed morning milking and would be frantic and miserable by now.

She rose, took a long drink of water, and went out to tend the animals. That done, she took stock of her place. She must get it into order for the next tenant. She didn't know how many days she would have before someone came to escort her to Yellaz.

So, the following day, and for many days thereafter, Ayia worked, eating little and sleeping less. She weeded the garden, harvested vegetables, and put up canned goods. She cleaned the house, sweeping dust and cobwebs out of corners and sorting her belongings. She found dark books among her collection that turned her thoughts toward the shadows after reading only the titles.

With a shudder, she bundled them into the yard and built a small bonfire. The reek of burning parchment and leather cleansed her spirit. While the fire was still hot, she went to her bedroom and found the light etching of Bryton's face. As she threw it into the flames with the books, she turned her face away so she wouldn't weaken and snatch it back out again.

When everything was clean, she sat and waited, wondering if she should walk to Luxa City and turn herself in. Or perhaps to Yellaz itself. Hodryk, if he lived, would be waiting for her. He would surely have named her Dark Spinner by now, if Keyar had not. He'd need another witness to corroborate; either Keyar or Quenlin could fulfill that requirement.

But she couldn't be sure anyone would come and care for the animals, so she stayed on, one more day, and then another and another. When her chores were done, she read her little book—or rather, Hodryk's little book—*The Founding of the*

Service, and longed for the days when she served the Creator and spun only light.

She tried to spin once, but her light was mixed with swirling colors, and she quenched it at once. Color was not forbidden, but playing with color had led her, once before, to experiment with a hint of darkness in her colors, and then to spin only the darkness. She didn't trust herself not to stray to that path again.

So, she didn't try to spin anymore. She let herself try to live, as if on borrowed time, merely in the physical world, discovering again its beauty all around her. She thought of Keyar often and longed to see his face. Longed to see him and feared to see him.

Then one day, nearly half a moon-cycle after Zeezia's death, as she hoed her garden, and the wind brought her the strong, sweet scent of zanna blossoms, and her chezoks bleated to call their young, she looked up and found Keyar and Quenlin watching her from the edge of the clearing.

Her heart skipped a beat and then thudded against her chest. It was time at last. She breathed deeply, taking in the sweet scent of the lush Luxeran landscape, a scent she might never enjoy again. Then she squared her shoulders and met the gaze, first of Keyar and then of Quenlin.

"Have you come to take me to Yellaz?" she asked.

She watched their faces, expecting grim agreement, censure, distaste at the task before them, but she saw only peace and determination.

"No, Aunt Ayia," Keyar said. Was that a smile that lurked in the corners of his mouth? "We've come to take you home."

Home? Wasn't she home now? But no, this little place was not home. It was just a waiting place. Looking to Quenlin for confirmation, she read in his expression that he knew this too.

"You've been alone long enough. Too long." Quenlin's eyes were clear, asking nothing, promising everything. "We can help you pack. I have room in my barns for your animals, if you want to bring them, or you can leave them for the next tenants."

Ayia glanced at Keyar. His face held no shadow of blame, no recriminations, only expectation. In the back of her mind, Yellaz still loomed, a fitting abode for someone who had slammed the book on a young girl's life. And beside it, an image formed of Quenlin's prosperous home, full of peace and welcome. She leaned on her hoe and stared at the two as they waited for her to speak.

She should run from them. Run straight to Yellaz. Tell them her story, her true story. But she was being offered something else. A different story. And a choice. She got to decide which would become the true story. These two, who loved her, were giving her this choice, and they stood still, waiting for her answer.

Light suffused the clearing. It grew moment by moment. It came from the sun, but it also emanated from Keyar and Quenlin. Looking down, Ayia was amazed to find it sparking from the ends of her own fingers, as well. She dropped her hoe and took a step toward the two waiting for her.

THE END

ABOUT EILEEN R HICKMAN

Eileen's favorite books are Fantasy or Science Fiction, so it was natural for her to start writing tales that bridge the divide between the two genres–a lot of Fantasy elements with a Science Fiction vibe. Her stories take place in her Seven World Dominion, and she delights in discovering new things about this many-faceted cosmos.

When she isn't writing and world-building, she's reading, making music, watching Star Trek, or traveling the world with camera in hand. She lives with her husband on the Colorado Front Range.

The foundation for her storytelling, and for everything else she does, is her faith in God. A committed Christ-follower, she seeks to honor him in all she does and in every story she tells.